The
Best
Native American
Myths, Legends,
and Folklore

Written and Edited by
G.W. Mullins
With Original Art by
C.L. Hause

ISBN: 978-1-64570-958-9

Second Edition Printing

Light Of The Moon Publishing has allowed this work to remain exactly as the author intended, verbatim, without editorial input.

Printed in the United States of America

The following book represents a collection of Native American works which are public domain. You may have read the stories before. In true story telling fashion, the stories have been left as close to the original form as possible. In Native American culture, in order to pass the stories along with all information intact, they had to be told pretty much word for word, to keep the legends alive. Many of these stories were translated directly from original Native language texts. With that in mind, please be aware that some spellings and word usage may vary from one tribe to another. For instance, the spelling of "teepee", as used in this book, can also be written as "tipi", and "tepee". All are correct. Also when using words like "someone", in most native cultures, it would be "some one". So keep in mind, these are not necessarily misspellings. They are simply dialect and translations.

<u>Other Titles Available From G.W. Mullins And C.L. Hause</u>

Walking With Spirits Native American Myths, Legends, And Folklore
Volumes One Thru Six

The Native American Cookbook

Native American Cooking - An Indian Cookbook With Legends And Folklore

The Native American Story Book - Stories Of The American Indians For Children
Volumes One Thru Five

The Best Native American Stories For Children

Cherokee A Collection of American Indian Legends, Stories And Fables

Creation Myths - Tales Of The Native American Indians

Strange Tales Of The Native American Indians

Spirit Quest - Stories Of The Native American Indians

Animal Tales Of The Native American Indians

Medicine Man - Shamanism, Natural Healing, Remedies And Stories Of The Native
American Indians

Native American Legends: Stories Of The Hopi Indians
Volumes One and Two

Totem Animals Of The Native Americans

The Best Native American Myths, Legends And Folklore
Volumes One Thru Three

Ghosts, Spirits And The Afterlife In Native American Indian Mythology And
Folklore

The Native American Art Book – Art Inspired By Native American Myths And
Legends

For information about the book and novel releases of
G.W. Mullins please visit his web site at
http://gwmullins.wix.com/books

All images contained in this book are original works by
C.L. Hause. For more information on his art and other projects
please visit his web page at *http://clarencehause.wix.com/homepage*

This book is dedicated to Vince Mullins, my Grandfather (Pawpaw). A tall red man who I loved so much. I think he would have liked this.

G.W. Mullins

All is Finished

I wanted to give something of my past to my grandson.
I told him that I would sing the sacred wolf song over him.
In my song, I appealed to the wolf to come and preside
over us, while I would perform the wolf ceremony.
So that the bondage between my grandson and the wolf
would be lifelong.
I sang.
In my voice was the hope that clings to every heartbeat.
I sang.
In my words were the powers I inherited from my
forefathers.
I sang.
In my cupped hands lay a spruce seed, the link to creation.
I sang.
In my eyes, sparkled love.
And the song floated on the sun's rays from tree to tree.
When I had ended, it was as if the whole world listened
with us to hear the wolf's reply.
We waited a long time but none came.
Again I sang, humbly but as invitingly as I could, until my
throat ached and my voice gave out.
All of a sudden I realized why no wolves had heard my
sacred song.
There were none left!
My heart filled with tears.
I could no longer give my grandson faith in the past, our
past.
I wept in silence.
All is finished!

...Chief Dan George (1899-1981)

Chief Dan George, (July 24, 1899 – September 23, 1981) was a chief of the Tsleil-Waututh Nation, a Coast Salish band located on Burrard Inlet in North Vancouver, British Columbia, Canada. He was also an author, poet, actor, and an Officer of the Order of Canada. At the age of 71, he was nominated for an Academy Award for Best Supporting Actor in Little Big Man.

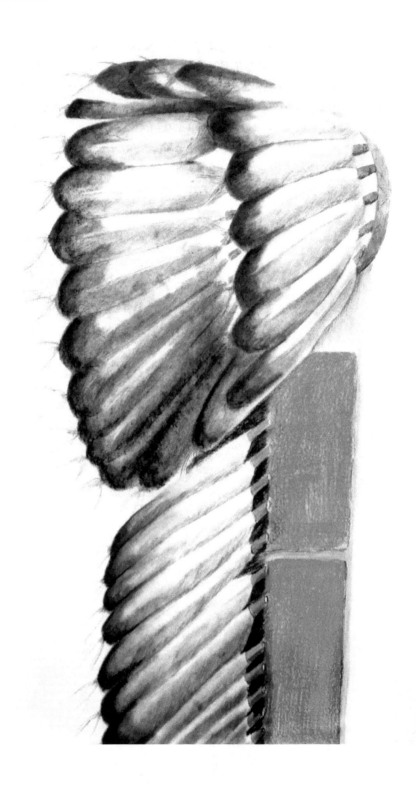

Table of Contents

Introduction

Before the time of books, computers, tablets and recording devices, the history of many cultures was passed down, from person to person, by word of mouth. The rich histories of so many people were told in songs, chants, poems and stories. This was and still is the way of Native American tribes. Each in its own way enriching their stories with their own experiences. By reliving these stories and songs, we have the opportunity to bring life back to the ancient spirits that created them. We have a chance to walk with the spirits of the past.

Native Americans used their stories to teach the children the traditions of their grandfathers. It was in this way that local customs were passed down and lessons were taught about how to live off the land and track animals. It was with stories they learned to grow crops and thrive in their natural environment.

When foreign men entered and settled upon Indian sacred lands, the Native Americans were often forcibly removed. They were sent to areas unfamiliar. If it were not for their customs, language and tradition passed down through stories, they would have lost connection with who they were. These songs and myths were their way of keeping their legacy alive.

Today Native Americans still keep their tribal languages alive. The myths and legends are still passed down from generation to generation.

Mythology

Mythology has always played a huge role in Native American stories. Of the stories told, those of Creation are often best known. Nature has always been looked at as an unfolding mystery. And in the stories of Native Americans, they sought to explain everything from natural occurrences, to animals, plant life, and weather related events. It was a way to express their ideas of their own beginnings.

Among all the stories told, each tribe had their own views of creation and how life came into this world. While some themes were similar, others could not be more different. In their stories, they explored the importance of Native American culture but also the individuality of each tribe and it's believes. These myths pay respect to the ancient ones that came before them and how nature has shaped their lives.

Songs, Poems and Music

Story telling didn't just involve words, or simple retelling of history. It included chants, poems, songs and music. Much set to the sound of a drum. The drumming invited everyone into the dance. After all, these stories and history were meant to be shared by all. It has been and still is custom to share stories and music at pow-wows.

Legacy

Through storytelling, the rich history of the Native American tribes is alive and well today. It has been shared and preserved and still pays tribute to fallen heroes of the past. Often, Native Americans have been misrepresented as violent people. It is through the glimpses into the past, and these stories much like the ones that are contained in this book, that you can see what a proud heritage they possess and how in tune with the Earth Native Americans really are.

Being there were so many different tribes with countless beliefs and customs, the only way to understand their ways is through understanding their stories. In this book I have endeavored to show a wide landscape of different tribes and hopefully present a true look at their beliefs.

With this book I hope you understand the Native American people a little better and understand where they have come from and what they can offer the world. By exploring these stories, I offer you a glimpse into an often forgotten past. The past of my people. I was born Cherokee and as a child heard many of these stories. These stories were passed to me in the old traditional way by my grandfather. And now I give these stories to you, to carry forward for younger generations to explore and learn.

Origin of the Pleiades

An Onondaga Legend

A long time ago a party of Indians went through the woods toward a good hunting-ground, which they had long known. They traveled several days through a very wild country, going on leisurely and camping by the way.

At last they reached Kan-ya-ti-yo, "the beautiful lake," where the gray rocks were crowned with great forest trees. Fish swarmed in the waters, and at every jutting point the deer came down from the hills around to bathe or drink of the lake. On the hills and in the valleys were huge beech and chestnut trees, where squirrels chattered, and bears came to take their morning and evening meals.

The chief of the band was Hah-yah-no, "Tracks in the water," and he halted his party on the lake shore that he might return thanks to the Great Spirit for their safe arrival at this good hunting-ground. "Here will we build our lodges for the winter, and may the Great Spirit, who has prospered us on our way, send us plenty of game, and health and peace." The Indian is always thankful.

The pleasant autumn days passed on. The lodges had been built, and hunting had prospered, when the children took a fancy to dance for their own amusement. They were getting lonesome, having little to do, and so they met daily in a quiet spot by the lake to have what they called their jolly dance. They had done this a long time, when one day a very old man came to them. They had seen no one like him before. He was dressed in white feathers, and his white hair shone like silver. His appearance was strange; his words were unpleasant as well. He told them they must stop their dancing, or evil would happen to them. Little did the children heed, for they were intent on their sport, and again and again the old man appeared, repeating his warning.

The mere dances did not afford all the enjoyment the children wished, and a little boy, who liked a good dinner, suggested a feast the next time they met. The food must come from their parents, and all were asked when they returned home. "You will waste and spoil good victuals," said one. "You can eat at home as you should," said another, and so they got nothing at all. Sorry as they were for this, they met and danced as before. A little to eat after each dance would have made them happy indeed. Empty stomachs cause no joy.

One day, as they danced, they found themselves rising little by little into the air, their heads being light through hunger. How this happened they did not know, but one said, "Do not look back, for something strange is taking place." A woman, saw them rise, and called them back, but with no effect, for they still rose slowly above the earth. She ran to the camp, and all rushed out with food of every kind, but the children would not return, though their parents called piteously after them. When one would look back he became a falling star. The others reached the sky, and are now what we call the Pleiades, and the Onondagas Oot-kwa-tah.

Every falling or shooting star recalls the story, but the seven stars shine on continuously, a pretty band of dancing children.

Only when the last tree has died and the last river been poisoned and the last fish been caught will we realize we cannot eat money.

~ Cree Indian Proverb ~

Grandmother Spider Steals the Fire

Choctaw

A Story of the Choctaw People of Tennessee and Mississippi

The Choctaw People say that when the People first came up out of the ground, People were encased in cocoons, their eyes closed, their limbs folded tightly to their bodies. And this was true of all People, the Bird People, the Animal People, the Insect People, and the Human People. The Great Spirit took pity on them and sent down someone to unfold their limbs, dry them off, and open their eyes. But the opened eyes saw nothing, because the world was dark, no sun, no moon, not even any stars.

All the People moved around by touch, and if they found something that didn't eat them first, they ate it raw, for they had no fire to cook it. All the People met in a great powwow, with the Animal and Bird People taking the lead, and the Human People hanging back. The Animal and Bird People decided that life was not good, but cold and miserable. A solution must be found! Someone spoke from the dark, "I have heard that the people in the East have fire." This caused a stir of wonder, "What could fire be?" There was a general discussion, and it was decided that if, as rumor had it, fire was warm and gave light, they should have it too. Another voice said, "But the people of the East are too greedy to share with us," So it was decided that the Bird and Animal People should steal what they needed, the fire!

But, who should have the honor? Grandmother Spider volunteered, "I can do it! Let me try!" But at the same time, Opossum began to speak. "I, Opossum, am a great chief of the animals. I will go to the East and since I am a great hunter, I will take the fire and hide it in the bushy hair on my tail." It was well known that Opossum had the furriest tail of all the animals, so he was selected.

When Opossum came to the East, he soon found the beautiful, red fire, jealously guarded by the people of the East. But Opossum got closer and closer until he picked up a small piece of burning wood, and stuck it in the hair of his tail, which promptly began to smoke, then flame. The people of the East said, "Look, that Opossum has stolen our fire!" They took it and put it back where it came from and drove Opossum away. Poor Opossum! Every bit of hair had burned from his tail, and to this day, opossums have no hair at all on their tails.

Once again, the powwow had to find a volunteer chief. Grandmother Spider again said, "Let me go! I can do it!" But this time a bird was elected, Buzzard. Buzzard was very proud. "I can succeed where Opossum has failed. I will fly to the East on my great wings, then hide the stolen fire in the beautiful long feathers on my head." The birds and animals still did not understand the nature of fire. So Buzzard flew to the East on his powerful wings, swooped past those defending the fire, picked up a small piece of burning ember, and hid it in his head feathers. Buzzard's head began to smoke and flame even faster! The people of the East said, "Look! Buzzard has stolen the fire!" And they took it and put it back where it came from.

Poor Buzzard! His head was now bare of feathers, red and blistered looking. And to this day, buzzards have naked heads that are bright red and blistered.

The powwow now sent Crow to look the situation over, for Crow was very clever. Crow at that time was pure white, and had the sweetest singing voice of all the birds. But he took so long standing over the fire, trying to find the perfect piece to steal that his white feathers were smoked black. And he breathed so much smoke that when he tried to sing, out came a harsh, "Caw! Caw!"

The Council said, "Opossum has failed. Buzzard and Crow have failed. Who shall we send?"

Tiny Grandmother Spider shouted with all her might, "LET ME TRY IT PLEASE!"

Though the council members thought Grandmother Spider had little chance of success, it was agreed that she should have her turn. Grandmother Spider looked then like she looks now, she had a small torso suspended by two sets of legs that turned the other way. She walked on all of her wonderful legs toward a stream where she had found clay. With those legs, she made a tiny clay container and a lid that fit perfectly with a tiny notch for air in the corner of the lid. Then she put the container on her back, spun a web all the way to the East, and walked tiptoe until she came to the fire. She was so small, the people from the East took no notice. She took a tiny piece of fire, put it in the container, and covered it with the lid. Then she walked back on tiptoe along the web until she came to the People. Since they couldn't see any fire, they said, "Grandmother Spider has failed."

"Oh no," she said, "I have the fire!" She lifted the pot from her back, and the lid from the pot, and the fire flamed up into its friend, the air. All the Birds and Animal People began to decide who would get this wonderful warmth. Bear said, "I'll take it!" but then he burned his paws on it and decided fire was not for animals, for look what happened to Opossum!

The Birds wanted no part of it, as Buzzard and Crow were still nursing their wounds. The insects thought it was pretty, but they, too, stayed far away from the fire.

Then a small voice said, "We will take it, if Grandmother Spider will help." The timid humans, whom none of the animals or birds thought much of, were volunteering!

So Grandmother Spider taught the Human People how to feed the fire sticks and wood to keep it from dying, how to keep the fire safe in a circle of stone so it couldn't escape and hurt them or their homes. While she was at it, she taught the humans about pottery made of clay and fire, and about weaving and spinning, at which Grandmother Spider was an expert.

The Choctaw remember. They made a beautiful design to decorate their homes, a picture of Grandmother Spider, two sets of legs up, two down, with a fire symbol on her back. This is so their children never forget to honor Grandmother Spider, Fire-bringer!

There is a road in the hearts of all of us, hidden and seldom traveled, which leads to an unknown, secret place.
The old people came literally to love the soil,
and they sat or reclined on the ground with a feeling of being close to a mothering power.
Their teepees were built upon the earth and their altars were made of earth.
The soul was soothing, strengthening, cleansing and healing.
That is why the old Indian still sits upon the earth instead of propping himself up and away from its life giving forces.
For him, to sit or lie upon the ground is to be able to think more deeply and to feel more keenly. He can see more clearly into the mysteries of life and come closer in kinship to other lives about him.

~ Chief Luther Standing Bear ~

The Lame Warrior
An Arapaho Legend

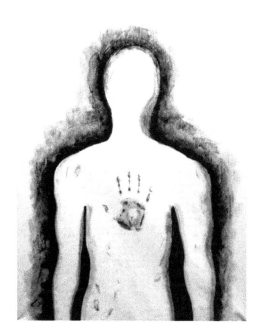

In the days before horses, a party of young Arapaho set off on foot one autumn morning in search of wild game in the western mountains. They carried heavy packs of food and spare moccasins, and one day as they were crossing the rocky bed of a shallow stream a young warrior felt a sudden sharp pain in his ankle. The ankle swelled and the pain grew worse until they pitched camp that night.

Next morning the warrior's ankle was swollen so badly that it was impossible for him to continue the journey with the others. His companions decided it was best to leave him. They cut young willows and tall grass to make a thatched shelter for him, and after the shelter was finished they collected a pile of dry wood so that he could keep a fire burning.

"When your ankle gets well," they told him, "don't try to follow us. Go back to our village, and await our return."

After several lonely days, the lame warrior tested his ankle, but it was still too painful to walk upon. And then one night a heavy snowstorm fell, virtually imprisoning him in the shelter. Because he had been unable to kill any wild game, his food supply was almost gone.

Late one afternoon he looked out and saw a large herd of buffalo rooting in the snow for grass quite close to his shelter. Reaching for his bow and arrow, he shot the fattest one and killed it. He then crawled out of the shelter to the buffalo, skinned it, and brought in the meat. After preparing a bed of coals, he placed a section of ribs in the fire for roasting.

Night had fallen by the time the ribs were cooked, and just as the lame warrior was reaching for a piece to eat, he heard footsteps crunching on the frozen snow. The steps came nearer and nearer to the closed flap of the shelter. "Who can that be?" he said to himself. "I am here alone and unable to run, but I shall defend myself if need be." He reached for his bow and arrow.

A moment later the flap opened and a skeleton clothed in a tanned robe stood there looking down at the lame warrior.

The robe was pinned tight at the neck so that only the skull was visible above and skeleton feet below. Frightened by this ghost, the warrior turned his eyes away from it.

"You must not be frightened of me," the skeleton said in a hoarse voice. "I have taken pity on you. Now you must take pity on me. Give me a piece of those roast ribs to eat, for I am very hungry."

Still very much alarmed by the presence of this unexpected visitor, the warrior offered a large piece of meat to an extended bony hand. He was astonished to see the skeleton chew the food with its bared teeth and swallow it.

"It was I who gave you the pain in your ankle," said the skeleton. "It was I who caused your ankle to swell so that you could not continue on the hunt. If you had gone on with your companions you would have been killed. The day they left you here, an enemy war party made a charge upon them, and they were all killed. I am the one who saved your life."

Again the skeleton's bony hand reached out, this time to rub the warrior's ankle. The pain and swelling vanished at once. "Now you can walk again," the ghost said. "Your enemies are all around, but if you will follow me I can lead you safely back to your village."

At dawn they left the shelter and started off across the snow, the skeleton leading the way. They walked through deep woods, along icy streams, and over high hills. Late in the afternoon the skeleton led the warrior up a steep ridge. When the warrior reached the summit, the ghost had vanished, but down in the valley below he could see the smokes of tepees in his Arapaho village.

"When you were born, you cried and the world rejoiced. Live your life so that when you die, the world cries and you rejoice."

Cherokee Expression

Origin of the Sweat Lodge
A Blackfoot Legend

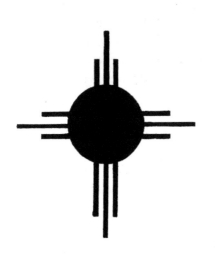

The Piegan tribe was southernmost at the headwaters of the Missouri River in Montana, a sub-tribe belonging to the Siksika Indians of North Saskatchewan in Canada. Piegans were of the Algonquian linguistic family, but warlike toward most of their neighboring tribes, since they had horses for raiding and were supplied with guns and ammunition by their Canadian sources. Piegans also displayed hostility toward explorers and traders. Several smallpox epidemics decimated their population. Now they are gathered on reservations on both sides of the border.

A girl of great beauty, the Chief's daughter, was worshipped by many young handsome men of the Piegan tribe. But she would not have any one of them for her husband.

One young tribesman was very poor and his face was marked with an ugly scar. Although he saw rich and handsome men of his tribe rejected by the Chief's daughter, he decided to find out if she would have him for her husband. When she laughed at him for even asking, he ran away toward the south in shame.

After traveling several days, he dropped to the ground, weary and hungry, and fell asleep. From the heavens, Morning-Star looked down and pitied the young unfortunate youth, knowing his trouble.

To Sun and Moon, his parents, Morning-Star said, "There is a poor young man lying on the ground with no one to help him. I want to go after him for a companion."

"Go and get him," said his parents.

Morning-Star carried the young man, Scarface, into the sky. Sun said, "Do not bring him into my lodge yet, for he smells ill. Build four sweat lodges."

When this was done, Sun led Scarface into the first sweat lodge. He asked Morning-Star to bring a hot coal on a forked stick. Sun then broke off a bit of sweet grass and placed it upon the hot coal. As the incense arose Sun began to sing, "Old Man is coming in with his body; it is sacred," repeating it four times.

Sun passed his hands back and forth through the smoke and rubbed them over the face, left arm, and side of Scarface. Sun repeated the ceremony on the boy's right side, purifying him and removing the odors of earthly people.

Sun took Scarface into the other three sweat lodges, performing the same healing ceremony. The body of Scarface changed color and he shone like a yellow light.

Using a soft feather, Sun brushed it over the youth's face, magically wiping away the scar. With a final touch to the young man's long, yellow hair, Sun caused him to look exactly like Morning-Star. The two young men were led by

Sun into his own lodge and placed side by side in the position of honor.

"Old Woman," called the father. "Which is your son?"

Moon pointed to Scarface, "That one is our son."

"You do not know your own child," answered Sun.

"He is not our son. We will call him Mistaken-for-Morning-Star," as they all laughed heartily at the mistake.

The two boys were together constantly and became close companions. One day, they were on an adventure when Morning-Star pointed out some large birds with very long, sharp beaks.

"Foster-Brother, I warn you not to go near those dangerous creatures," said Morning-Star. "They killed my other brothers with their beaks."

Suddenly the birds chased the two boys. Morning-Star fled toward his home, but Foster-Brother stopped, picking up a club and one by one struck the birds dead.

Upon reaching home, Morning-Star excitedly reported to his father what had happened. Sun made a victory song honoring the young hero. In gratitude for saving Morning-Star's life, Sun gave him the forked stick for lifting hot embers and a braid of sweet grass to make incense. These sacred elements necessary for making the sweat lodge ceremony were a gift of trust.

"And this my sweat lodge I give to you," said the Sun. Mistaken-for-Morning-Star observed very carefully how it was constructed, in his mind preparing himself to one day returning to earth.

When Scarface did arrive at his tribal village, all of his people gathered to see the handsome young man in their midst. At first, they did not recognize him as Scarface.

"I have been in the sky," he told them. "Behold me, Morning-Star looks just like this. The Sun gave me these things used in the sweat lodge healing ceremony. That is how I lost my ugly scar."

Scarface explained how the forked stick and sweet grass were used. Then he set to work showing his people how to make the sweat lodge. This is how the first medicine sweat lodge was built upon earth by the Piegan tribe.

Now that Scarface was so very handsome and brought such a great blessing of healing to his tribe, the Chief's beautiful daughter became his wife.

In remembrance of Sun's gift to Scarface and his tribe, the Piegans always make the sweat lodge healing ceremony an important part of their annual Sun Dance Celebration.

Inuit Story of the Northern Lights
An Eskimo Legend

Auroras - or Northern Lights - are believed to be the torches held in the hands of Spirits seeking the souls of those who have just died, to lead them over the abyss terminating the edge of the world. A narrow pathway leads across it to the land of brightness and plenty, where disease and pain are no more, and where food of all kinds is already in abundance. To this place none but the dead and the Raven can go. When the Spirits wish to communicate with the people of the Earth, they make a whistling noise, and the Earth people answer only in a whispering tone. The Eskimo say that they are able to call the Aurora and converse with it. They send messages to the dead through these Spirits.

It is the general belief of the Indians that after a man dies his spirit is somewhere on the earth or in the sky, we do not know exactly where, but we are sure that his spirit still lives. . . . So it is with Wakantanka. We believe that he is everywhere, yet he is to us as the spirits of our friends, whose voices we can not hear.

Chased-by-Bears, Santee-Yanktonai Sioux

The Legend of the Cherokee Rose

Cherokee Legend

In the latter half of 1838, Cherokee People who had not voluntarily moved west earlier were forced to leave their homes in the East.

The trail to the West was long and treacherous and many were dying along the way. The People's hearts were heavy with sadness and their tears mingled with the dust of the trail.

The Elders knew that the survival of the children depended upon the strength of the women. One evening around the campfire, the Elders called upon Heaven Dweller, *ga lv la di e hi*. They told Him of the People's suffering and tears. They were afraid the children would not survive to rebuild the Cherokee Nation.

Gal v la di e hi spoke to them, "To let you know how much I care, I will give you a sign. In the morning, tell the women to look back along the trail. Where their tears have fallen, I will cause to grow a plant that will have seven leaves for the seven clans of the Cherokee. Amidst the plant will be a delicate white rose with five petals. In the center of the blossom will be a pile of gold to remind the Cherokee of the white man's greed for the gold found on the Cherokee homeland. This plant will be sturdy and strong with stickers on all the stems. It will defy anything which tries to destroy it."

The next morning the Elders told the women to look back down the trail. A plant was growing fast and covering the trail where they had walked. As the women watched, blossoms formed and slowly opened. They forgot their sadness. Like the plant the women began to feel strong and beautiful. As the plant protected its blossoms, they knew they would have the courage and determination to protect their children who would begin a new Nation in the West.

Sunset. Then I was standing on the highest mountain of them all, and round about beneath me was the whole hoop of the world. And while I stood there I saw more than I can tell and I understood more than I saw; for I was seeing in a sacred manner the shapes of all things in the spirit, and the shape of all shapes as they must live together like one being.

And I say the sacred hoop of my people was one of the many hoops that made one circle, wide as daylight and as starlight, and in the center grew one mighty flowering tree to shelter all the children of one mother and one father. And I saw that it was holy...

But anywhere is the center of the world.

- Black Elk 3

The Legend of the Dream Catcher

The Old Ones tell that dreams hold great power and drift about at night before coming to the sleeping ones.

To keep the dreamer safe, the Old Ones created a special web, the Dream Catcher, to hang above their sleeping places. When dreams traveled the web paths, the bad dreams lost their way and became entangled, disappearing with the first rays of daybreak, like the morning dew on the grass. The good dreams, knowing their way, passed through the center and were guided gently to the sleeping ones.

An old Sioux Indian legend says that dream catchers were hung in lodges and teepees to ensure peaceful dreams. The good dreams, knowing the way, slip through the webbing and slide down the soft feather to the sleeper. The bad dreams, not knowing the way, become entangled in the web, and melt at the first light of the new day. Small dream catchers were hung on cradleboards, so that infants would have only good dreams.

The Bear Man
Cherokee Legend

One springtime morning a Cherokee named Whirlwind told his wife goodbye and left his village to go up in the Smoky Mountains to hunt for wild game. In the forest he saw a black bear and wounded it with an arrow. The bear turned and started to run away, but the hunter followed, shooting one arrow after another into the animal without bringing it down. Whirlwind did not know that this bear possessed secret powers, and could talk and read the thoughts of people.

At last the black bear stopped and pulled the arrows out of his body and gave them to Whirlwind. "It is of no use for you to shoot at me," he said. "You can't kill me. Come with me and I will show you how bears live."

"This bear may kill me," Whirlwind said to himself, but the bear read his thoughts and said, "No, I will not hurt you."

"How can I get anything to eat if I go with this bear," Whirlwind thought, and again the bear knew what the hunter was thinking, and said, "I have plenty of food."

Whirlwind decided to go with the bear. They walked until they came to a cave in the side of a mountain, and the bear said, "This is not where I live, but we are holding a council here and you can see what we do." They entered the cave, which widened as they went farther in until it was as large as a Cherokee long house. It was filled with bears, old and young, brown and black, and one large white bear, who was the chief. Whirlwind sat down in a corner beside the black bear who had brought him inside, but soon the other bears scented his presence.

"What is that bad smell of a man?" one asked, but the bear chief answered, "Don't talk so. It is only a stranger come to see us. Let him alone."

The bears began to talk among themselves, and Whirlwind was astonished that he could understand what they were saying. They were discussing the scarcity of food of all kinds in the mountains, and were trying to decide what to do about it. They had sent messengers in all directions, and two of them had returned to report on what they had found. In a valley to the south, they said, was a large stand of chestnuts and oaks, and the ground beneath them was covered with mast. Pleased at this news, a huge black bear named Long Hams announced he would lead them in a dance.

While they were dancing, the bears noticed Whirlwind's bow and arrows, and Long Hams stopped and said, "This is what men use to kill us. Let us see if we can use them. Maybe we can fight them with their own weapons."

Long Hams took the bow and arrows from Whirlwind. He fitted an arrow and drew back the sinew string, but when he let go, the string caught in his long claws and the arrow fell to the ground. He saw that he could not use the bow and arrows and gave them back to Whirlwind. By this time, the bears had finished their dance, and were leaving the cave to go to their separate homes.

Whirlwind went out with the black bear who had brought him there, and after a long walk they came to a smaller cave in the side of the mountain. "This is where I live," the bear said, and led the way inside. Whirlwind could see no food anywhere in the cave, and wondered how he was going to get something to satisfy his hunger. Reading his thoughts, the bear sat up on his hind legs and made a movement with his forepaws. When he held his paws out to Whirlwind they were filled with chestnuts. He repeated this magic and his paws were filled with huckleberries which he gave to Whirlwind. He then presented him with blackberries, and finally some acorns.

"I cannot eat acorns," Whirlwind said. "Besides, you have given me enough to eat already."

For many moons, through the summer and winter, Whirlwind lived in the cave with the bear. After a while he noticed that his hair was growing all over his body like that of a bear. He learned to eat acorns and act like a bear, but he still walked upright like a man.

On the first warm day of spring the bear told Whirlwind that he had dreamed of the Cherokee village down in the valley. In the dream he heard the Cherokees talking of a big hunt in the mountains.

"Is my wife still waiting there for me?" Whirlwind asked.

"She awaits your return," the bear replied. "But you have become a bear man. If you return you must shut yourself out of sight of your people for seven days without food or drink. At the end of that time you will become like a man again."

A few days later a party of Cherokee hunters came up into the mountains. The black bear and Whirlwind hid themselves in the cave, but the hunters' dogs found the entrance and began to bark furiously.

"I have lost my power against arrows," the bear said. "Your people will kill me and take my skin from me, but they will not harm you. They will take you home with them. Remember what I told you, if you wish to lose your bear nature and become a man again." The Cherokee hunters began throwing lighted pine knots inside the cave.

"They will kill me and drag me outside and cut me in pieces," the bear said. "Afterwards you must cover my blood with leaves. When they are taking you away, if you look back you will see something."

As the bear had foretold, the hunters killed him with arrows and dragged his body outside and took the skin from it and cut the meat into quarters to carry back to their village. Fearing that they might mistake him for another bear, Whirlwind remained in the cave, but the dogs continued barking at him. When the hunters looked inside, they saw a hairy man standing upright, and one of them recognized Whirlwind.

Believing that he had been a prisoner of the bear, they asked him if he would like to go home with them and try to rid himself of his bear nature. Whirlwind replied that he would go with them, but explained that he would have to stay alone in a house for seven days without food or water in order to become as a man again.

While the hunters were loading the meat on their backs, Whirlwind piled leaves over the place where they had killed the bear, carefully covering the drops of blood. After they had walked a short distance down the mountain, Whirlwind looked behind him. He saw a bear rise up out of the leaves, shake himself, and go back into the cave.

When the hunters reached their village, they took Whirlwind to an empty house, and obeying his wishes, barred the entrance door. Although he asked them to say nothing to anyone of his hairiness and his bear nature, one of the hunters must have told of his presence in the village because the very next morning Whirlwind's wife heard that he was there.

She hurried to see the hunters and begged them to let her see her long missing husband.

"You must wait for seven days," the hunters told her. "Come back after seven days, and Whirlwind will return to you as he was when he left the village twelve moons ago."

Bitterly disappointed, the woman went away, but she returned to the hunters each day, pleading with them to let her see her husband. She begged so hard that on the fifth day they took her to the house, unfastened the door, and told Whirlwind to come outside and let his wife see him.

Although he was still hairy and walked like a bear on hind legs, Whirlwind's wife was so pleased to see him again that she insisted he come home with her. Whirlwind went with her, but a few days later he died, and the Cherokees knew that the bears had claimed him because he still had a bear's nature and could not live like a man. If they had kept him shut up in the house without food until the end of the seven days he would have become like a man again. And that is why in that village on the first warm and misty nights of springtime, the ghosts of two bears -- one walking on all fours, the other walking upright -- are still seen to this day.

Children were encouraged to develop strict discipline and a high regard for sharing.

When a girl picked her first berries and dug her first roots, they were given away to an elder so she would share her future success.

When a child carried water for the home, an elder would give compliments, pretending to taste meat in water carried by a boy or berries in that of a girl.

The child was encouraged not to be lazy and to grow straight like a sapling.

- Mourning Dove (1888-1936)

Dreams are not just for the young. They are for children of all ages. To dream is to live, without our dreams we will cease to live and merely exist. Dare to dream and live!

Unknown

The First Moccisons

There was once a great chief on the Plains who had very
tender feet. Other mighty chiefs laughed at him; little chiefs
only smiled as he hobbled past; and though they did not
dare to smile, the people of the tribe also enjoyed the big
chief's discomfort. All of them were in the same canoe,
having no horses and only bare feet, but luckily very few of
them had tender feet. The unhappy medicine man who was
advisor to the Chief-of-the-Tender-Feet was afraid and
troubled. Each time he was called before the chief he was
asked, 'What are you going to do about it?" The 'it' meant
the chief's tender feet.

Forced by fear, the medicine man at last hit upon a plan.
Though he knew that it was not the real answer to the
chief's foot problem, nevertheless it was a good makeshift.
The medicine man had some women of the tribe weave a
long, narrow mat of reeds, and when the big chief had to go
anywhere, four braves unrolled the mat in front of him so
that he walked in comfort. One day, the braves were worn
out from seeing that the chief's feet were not worn out.

They carelessly unrolled the mat over a place where flint arrowheads had been chipped. The arrowheads had long ago taken flight, but the needle-sharp chips remained. When the big chief's tender feet were wounded by these chips, he uttered a series of whoops which made the nearby aspen tree leaves quiver so hard that they have been trembling ever since.

That night the poor medicine man was given an impossible task by the angry chief: 'Cover the whole earth with mats so thick that my feet will not suffer. If you fail, you will die when the moon is round.'

The frightened maker of magic crept back to his lodge. He did not wish to be put to death on the night of the full moon, but he could think of no way to avoid it. Suddenly he saw the hide of an elk which he had killed pegged to the ground, with two women busily scraping the hair from the hide, and an idea flashed into his groping mind. He sent out many hunters; many women were busy for many days; many braves with hunting knives cut, and women sewed with bone needles and rawhide sinews.

On the day before the moon was round, the medicine man went to the chief and told him that he had covered as much of the earth as was possible in so short a time. When the chief looked from the door of his lodge, he saw many paths of skin stretching as far as he could see. Long strips which could be moved from place to place connected the main leather paths. Even the chief thought that this time the magic of the medicine man had solved tenderfoot transportation for all time - but this was not to be!

One day, as the big chief was walking along one of his smooth, tough leather paths, he saw a pretty maiden of the tribe gliding ahead of him, walking on the hard earth on one side of the chief's pathway. She glanced back when she heard the pitter- patter of his feet on the elk hide pathway and seemed to smile. The chief set off on the run to catch up with her, his eyes fixed on the back of She-Who-Smiled, and so his feet strayed from the narrow path and landed in a bunch of needle-sharp thorns! The girl ran for her life when she heard the hideous howls of the chief, and Indians in the distant village thought that they were being attacked by wildcats.

Two suns later, when the chief was calm enough to speak again, he had his medicine man brought before him and told the unhappy man that next day, when the sun was high, he would be sent with all speed to the land of shadows.

That night, the medicine man climbed to the top of a high hill in search of advice from friendly spirits on how to cover the entire earth with leather. He slept, and in a dream vision he was shown the answer to his problem. Amid vivid flashes of lightning, he tore down the steep hillside, howling louder than the big chief at times, as jagged rocks wounded his bare feet and legs. He did not stop until he was safely inside his lodge. He worked all night and until the warriors who were to send him on the shadow trail came for him, just before noon the next day. He was surrounded by the war-club armed guards. He was clutching close to his heart something tightly rolled in a piece of deerskin. His cheerful smile surprised those who saw him pass. 'Wah, he is brave!' said the men of the tribe. 'He is very brave!' said the women of the tribe.

The big chief was waiting just outside his lodge. He gave the guards swift, stern orders. Before the maker of magic could be led away, he asked leave to say a few words to the chief. 'Speak!' said the chief, sorry to lose a clever medicine man who was very good at most kinds of magic. Even the chief knew that covering the entire earth with leather was an impossible task.

The medicine man quickly knelt beside the chief, unrolled the two objects which he took from his bundle and slipped one of them on each foot of the chief. The chief seemed to be wearing a pair of bear's hairless feet, instead of bare feet, and he was puzzled at first as he looked at the elk hide handicraft of his medicine man. 'Big chief,' the medicine man exclaimed joyfully, 'I have found the way to cover the earth with leather! For you, O chief, from now on the earth will always be covered with leather.' And so it was.

Conversation was never begun at once, nor in a hurried manner. No one was quick with a question, no matter how important, and no one was pressed for an answer. A pause giving time for thought was the truly courteous way of beginning and conducting a conversation. Silence was meaningful with the Lakota, and his granting a space of silence to the speech-maker and his own moment of silence before talking was done in the practice of true politeness and regard for the rule that "thought comes before speech."

Luther Standing Bear, Oglala Sioux Chief

The Gift of the Peace Pipe

One day, two young men were hunting wild game for their village. There were not many large game in the region and the people were hungry. While wading through snowdrifts among the trees, they were startled to see a beautiful young woman standing before them. She was dressed in pretty robes, and in her hand she held a small bundle. The young men could not think of anything to say, so they just stood and looked at her.

"Do not fear," said the woman, "I bring you peace and happiness. Now tell me, why are you so far from your village?"

Her grace and beauty so fired the older brave with love that he could not speak. Finally, the younger man spoke.

"Our village is in need of more food," he said. "We are hunting."

"Here," she said, "take this bundle back to your people. Tell the Chiefs of the seven campfires to meet in the council lodge and wait for me."

The two men still could think of nothing to say. The older brave, blinded by love for the beautiful woman, reached out to touch her. As he did so, she touched him lightly on the head and he fell to the ground. A cloud enveloped his body, and all that was left of him was a pile of white bones. Then, as suddenly as she appeared, she disappeared.

The younger brave realized that his companion had "evil thoughts" about the woman, and that's why he was punished. He then hurried back to the village to tell the Chiefs. The next day the seven Chiefs put on their best feathers and robes and sat in a circle, all looking down at the bundle which had not been opened.

A sudden blow of wind passed. When it had gone the Chiefs saw before them a beautiful woman dressed in pretty robes. None of them could find words in their mouths. So she spoke to them:

"I bring you a message of peace. Your people are great hunters and brave warriors. When the sun rises again, pack your belongings and travel toward the setting sun. There a great land awaits you. You will find beyond the Father of Waters new animals and other tribes of people. In this bundle is a pipe to bring you peace with all the people."

The woman took out a pipe made from bone and decorated with bird feathers. Then she left the lodge and disappeared.

Soon the tribes moved westward. They came to the Mississippi River which was called the Father of Waters, and then to the Missouri River and the Black Hills. They saw for the first time the animals we call horses, and there were great herds of buffalo.

To make peace with the other tribes, the Sioux chieftains brought out their peace pipe. The pipe was usually handed to the Chief of the enemy tribe first and then it was smoked by all the leaders of both tribes. Later, when the white men came to the Sioux country, the Indians brought out their pipe of peace to smoke, but the white men would not smoke it.

A great amount of soft red stone was found for making pipes and every year all the Sioux tribes would send some of their people to the pipestone quarries to smoke the pipe of peace with other tribes. This place came to be known as Pipestone, the name which it carries to this day as a town and Indian school in Minnesota.

A Sioux once said, "The pipe is us. The stem is our backbone, the bowl our head, the stone our blood, red as our skin."

Pipes are among the most sacred objects to the Lakota being used in ceremonies. The more decorated the pipe -- the stronger its powers.

A very great vision is needed and the man who has it must follow it as the eagle seeks the deepest blue of the sky.

- Crazy Horse, Oglala Lakota Sioux (circa 1840-1877)

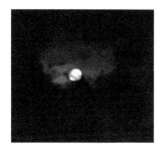

Brother of the Moon
Cherokee

As the Cherokee's conception of Christ did not fit any European style Christmas ceremony and the fact that we, the Tsa la gi have been upon this earth a long, long time, we had our own ways of celebrating and giving thanks. Since back then, the ways have changed; however some things stay the same. The seasons don't change, the significance of 4 stays the same and that of 7 also does not change. It can be said that the celebrations were held this way or that but we were not there and these are closely guarded secrets. Perhaps they will be shared when the time is right perhaps, if we were there at a celebration of long ago at this time of the changing of seasons it would have gone something like this:

It is the time of change when the leaves are red and upon the earth and the bare branches of the trees sigh a bit of relief to shed their burden. The winter coats are thick and warm on the creatures of our mother Our brother the Bear is in the womb of earth mother contemplating the coming seasons and dreaming of ripe berries. The old man of the North has blanketed the earth mother with a fresh coat of snow and the promise of regeneration lies just below it. It is the time of the changing of seasons from the time of harvesting to winter and the time to give thanks for the year we have had and the year to come.

As the spirit world is the most powerful at dawn or sunrise the ceremony will be at sunrise. The villagers gather at the sacred fire pit and the keeper of the sacred fire adds the ashes from the previous fire to this and the fire glows. This insures the circle continues from one fire to the next, from one season to the other from one generation to the next.

A man of medicine leads us in our prayers, song and thanks. He speaks his silent prayer asking the spirits of the 4 directions to help him carry the prayers to the creator. He asks the sun father and star nation of the skies to also help carry the prayers of thanks. He asks the mother of us all to give her blessing and help carry the prayers and for the Tsa la gi, the 7th spirit. Sometimes called in different ways it is the power within us, the power around us it is that of our beings our own spirit, it is also asked to help carry our prayers and bless us this day.

As the sun rises and we stand facing the east we sing. We sing a song of welcome to the sun and we pray. It is time to thank the creator for the food stores that will get us thru the winter and to thank the creatures of the earth for giving their lives so that we and our families may live. It is time to thank the earth mother for being good to us and for the plant people she provides us that heal and nourish us.

We pray around the fire and give thanks for all these things and we pray for the coming year and that it may be good to the earth mother. For if it is good to her, it will be good for us and the creatures of the earth. We also at this time thank the Corn Mothers for providing us with her corn, which is a large part of our daily nourishment. We share grits passed to show that we are grateful and to forgive the things of the past. We will sing and pray and perhaps dance this day, as we are grateful to the spirits and show our love for the earth and one another. It is another passing of the seasons.

One more way we give thanks near this day called Christmas.

How the Milky Way Came to Be
A Cherokee Legend

Long ago when the world was young, there were not many stars in the sky.

In those days the people depended on corn for their food. Dried corn could be made into corn meal by placing it inside a large hollowed stump and pounding it with a long wooden pestle. The cornmeal was stored in large baskets. During the winter, the ground meal could be made into bread and mush.

One morning an old man and his wife went to their storage basket for some cornmeal. They discovered that someone or something had gotten into the cornmeal during the night. This upset them very much for no one in a Cherokee village stole from someone else.

Then they noticed that the cornmeal was scattered over the ground. In the middle of the spilt meal were giant dog prints. These dog prints were so large that the elderly couple knew this was no ordinary dog.

They immediately alerted the people of the village. It was decided that this must be a spirit dog from another world. The people did not want the spirit dog coming to their village. They decided to get rid of the dog by frightening it so bad it would never return. They gathered their drums and turtle shell rattles and later that night they hid around the area where the cornmeal was kept.

Late into the night they heard a whirring sound like many bird wings. They look up to see the form of a giant dog swooping down from the sky. It landed near the basket and then began to eat great mouthfuls of cornmeal.

Suddenly the people jumped up beating and shaking their noise makers. The noise was so loud it sounded like thunder. The giant dog turned and began to run down the path. The people chased after him making the loudest noises they could. It ran to the top of a hill and leaped into the sky, the cornmeal spilling out the sides of its mouth.

The giant dog ran across the black night sky until it disappeared from sight. But the cornmeal that had spilled from its mouth made a path way across the sky. Each gain of cornmeal became a star.

The Cherokees call that pattern of stars, gi li' ut sun stan un' yi (gil-LEE-oot-soon stan-UNH-yee), "the place where the dog ran."

And that is how the Milky Way came to be.

The Story of the Drum
An Abenaki Legend

It is said that when Creator was giving a place for all the spirits to dwell who would be taking part in the inhabitance of Mother Earth, there came a sound, a loud BOOM, from off in the distance.

As Creator listened, the sound kept coming closer and closer until it finally it was right in front of Creator. "Who are you?" asked Creator. "I am the spirit of the drum" was the reply. I have come here to ask you to allow me to take part in this wonderful thing." "How will you take part?" Creator questioned." I would like to accompany the singing of the people. When they sing from their hearts, I will to sing as though I was the heartbeat of Mother Earth. In that way, all creation will sing in harmony. "Creator granted the request, and from then on, the drum accompanied the people's voices.

Throughout all of the indigenous peoples of the world, the drum is the center of all songs. It is the catalyst for the spirit of the songs to rise up to the Creator so that the prayers in those songs reach where they were meant to go. At all times, the sound of the drum brings completeness, awe, excitement, solemnity, strength, courage, and the fulfillment to the songs. It is Mother's heartbeat giving her approval to those living upon her. It draws the eagle to it, which carries the message to Creator.

Ghost of the White Deer

Chickasaw
A lore of the Chickasaw People of Oklahoma

A brave, young warrior for the Chickasaw Nation fell in love with the daughter of a chief. The chief did not like the young man, who was called Blue Jay. So the chief invented a price for the bride that he was sure that Blue Jay could not pay.

"Bring me the hide of the White Deer," said the chief. The Chickasaws believed that animals that were all white were  magical. "The price for my daughter is one white deer." Then the chief laughed. The chief knew that an all white deer, an albino, was very rare and would be very hard to find. White deerskin was the best material to use in a wedding dress, and the best white deer skin came from the albino deer.

Blue Jay went to his beloved, whose name was Bright Moon. "I will return with your bride price in one moon, and we will be married. This I promise you." Taking his best bow and his sharpest arrows Blue Jay began to hunt.

Three weeks went by, and Blue Jay was often hungry, lonely, and scratched by briars. Then, one night during a full moon, Blue Jay saw a white deer that seemed to drift through the moonlight. When the deer was very close to where Blue Jay hid, he shot his sharpest arrow. The arrow sank deep into the deer's heart. But instead of sinking to his knees to die, the deer began to run. And instead of running away, the deer began to run toward Blue Jay, his red eyes glowing, his horns sharp and menacing.

A month passed and Blue Jay did not return as he had promised Bright Moon. As the months dragged by, the tribe decided that he would never return.

But Bright Moon never took any other young man as a husband, for she had a secret. When the moon was shining as brightly as her name, Bright Moon would often see the white deer in the smoke of the campfire, running, with an arrow in his heart. She lived hoping the deer would finally fall, and Blue Jay would return.

To this day the white deer is sacred to the Chickasaw People, and the white deerskin is still the favorite material for the wedding dress.

Mooin, the Bear's Child

Now in the Old Time there lived a boy called Sigo, whose father had died when he was a baby. Sigo was too young to hunt and provide food for the wigwam, so his mother was obliged to take another husband, a jealous spiteful man who soon came to dislike his small stepson, for he thought the mother cared more for the child than for himself. He thought of a plan to be rid of the boy.

"Wife," said he, "it is time the boy learned something of the forest. I will take him with me today, hunting."

"Oh no!" cried his wife. "Sigo is far too young!"

But the husband snatched the boy and took him into the forest, while the mother wept, for she knew her husband's jealous heart.

The stepfather knew of a cave deep in the forest, a deep cave that led into a rocky hill. To this cave, he led his stepson and told him to go inside and hunt for the tracks of rabbit. The boy hung back.

"It is dark in there. I am afraid."

"Afraid!" scoffed the man. "A fine hunter you'll make," and he pushed the boy roughly into the cave. "Stay in there until I tell you to come out."

Then the stepfather took a pole and thrust it under a huge boulder so that it tumbled over and covered the mouth of the cave completely. He knew well there was no other opening. The boy was shut in for good and would soon die of starvation.

The stepfather left the place, intending to tell the boy's mother that her son had been disobedient, had run off and got lost, and he had been unable to find him. He would not return home at once. He would let time pass, as if he had been looking for the boy. Another idea occurred to him. He would spend the time on Blomidon's beach and collect some of Glooscap's purple stones to take as a peace offering to his wife. She might suspect, but nothing could be proved, and nobody would ever know what had happened.

Nobody? There was one who knew already. Glooscap the Great Chief was well aware of what had happened and he was angry, very angry. He struck his great spear into the red stone of Blomidon and the clip split. Earth and stones tumbled down, down, down to the beach, burying the wicked stepfather and killing him instantly.

Then Glooscap called upon a faithful servant, Porcupine, and told him what he was to do.

In the dark cave in the hillside, Sigo cried out his loneliness and fear. He was only six after all, and he wanted his mother. Suddenly he heard a voice.

"Sigo! Come this way."

He saw two glowing eyes and went towards them, trembling. The eyes grew bigger and brighter and at last he could see they belonged to an old porcupine.

"Don't cry any more, my son," said Porcupine. "I am here to help you," and the boy was afraid no longer. He watched as Porcupine went to the cave entrance and tried to push away the stone, but the stone was too heavy. Porcupine put his lips to the crack of light between boulder and hill side and called out:

"Friends of Glooscap! Come around, all of you!"

The animals and birds heard him and came--Wolf, Raccoon, Caribou, Turtle, Possum, Rabbit, and Squirrel, and birds of all kinds from Turkey to Hummingbird.

"A boy has been left here to die," called the old Porcupine from inside the cave. "I am not strong enough to move the rock. Help us or we are lost."

The animals called back that they would try. First Raccoon marched up and tried to wrap his arms around the stone, but they were much too short. Then Fox came and bit and scratched at the boulder, but he only made his lips bleed. Then Caribou stepped up and, thrusting her long antlers into the crack, she tried to pry the stone loose, but only broke off one of her antlers. It was no use. In the end, all gave up. They could not move the stone.

"Kwah-ee," a new voice spoke. "What is going on?" They turned and saw Mooinskw, which means she-bear, who had come quietly out of the woods. Some of the smaller animals were frightened and hid, but the others told Mooinskw what had happened. She promptly embraced the boulder in the cave's mouth and heaved with all her great strength. With a rumble and a crash, the stone rolled over. Then out came Sigo and Porcupine, joyfully.

Porcupine thanked the animals for their help and said, "Now I must find someone to take care of this boy and bring him up. My food is not the best for him. Perhaps there is someone here whose diet will suit him better. The boy is hungry--who will bring him food?"

All scattered at once in search of food. Robin was the first to return, and he laid down worms before the boy, but Sigo could not eat them. Beaver came next, with bark, but the boy shook his head. Others brought seeds and insects, but Sigo, hungry as he was, could not touch any of them, At last came Mooinskw and held out a flat cake made of blue berries. The boy seized it eagerly and ate.

"Oh, how good it is," he cried. And Porcupine nodded wisely.

"From now on," he said, "Mooinskw will be this boy's foster mother."

So Sigo went to live with the bears. Besides the mother bear, there were two boy cubs and a girl cub. All were pleased to have a new brother and they soon taught Sigo all their tricks and all the secrets of thee forest, and Sigo was happy with his new-found family. Gradually, he forgot his old life. Even the face of his mother grew dim in memory and, walking often on all fours as the bears did, he almost began to think he was a bear.

One spring when Sigo was ten, the bears went fishing for smelts. Mooinskw walked into the water, seated herself on her haunches and commenced seizing the smelts and tossing them out on the bank to the children. All were enjoying themselves greatly when suddenly Mooinskw plunged to the shore, crying, "Come children, hurry!" She had caught the scent of man. "Run for your lives!"

As they ran, she stayed behind them, guarding them, until at last they were safe at home.

"What animal was that, Mother?" asked Sigo.

"That was a hunter," said his foster-mother, "a human like yourself, who kills bears for food." And she warned them all to be very watchful from now on. "You must always run from the sight or scent of a hunter."

Not long afterwards, the bear family went with other bear families to pick blueberries for the winter. The small ones soon tired of picking and the oldest cub had a sudden mischievous thought.

"Chase me towards the crowd," he told Sigo, "just as men do when they hunt bears. The others will be frightened and run away. Then we can have all the berries for ourselves."

So Sigo began to chase his brothers towards the other bears, whooping loudly, and the bears at once scattered in all directions. All, that is, except the mother bear who recognized the voice of her adopted son.

"Offspring of Lox!" she cried. "What mischief are you up to now?" And she rounded up the children and spanked them soundly, Sigo too.

So the sun crossed the sky each day and the days grew shorter. At last the mother bear led her family to their winter quarters in a large hollow tree. For half the winter they were happy and safe, with plenty of blueberry cakes to keep them from being hungry. Then, one sad day, the hunters found the tree.

Seeing the scratches on its trunk, they guessed that bears were inside, and they prepared to smoke them out into the open.

Mooinskw knew well enough what was about to happen and that not all would escape.

"I must go out first," she said, "and attract the man's attention, while you two cubs jump out and run away. Then you, Sigo, show yourself and plead for your little sister. Perhaps they will spare her for your sake."

And thus it happened, just as the brave and loving mother bear had said. As soon as she climbed down from the tree, the Indians shot her dead, but the two male cubs had time to escape. Then Sigo rushed out, crying:

"I am a human, like you. Spare the she-cub, my adopted sister."

The amazed Indians put down their arrows and spears and, when they had heard Sigo's story, they gladly spared the little she-bear and were sorry they had killed Mooinskw who had been so good to an Indian child.

Sigo wept over the body of his foster mother and made a solemn vow.

"I shall be called Mooin, the bear's son, from this day forwards. And when I am grown, and a hunter, never will I kill a mother bear, or bear children!"

And Mooin never did.

With his foster sister, he returned to his old village, to the great joy of his Indian mother, who cared tenderly for the she-cub until she was old enough to care for herself.

And ever since then, when Indians see smoke rising from a hollow tree, they know a mother bear is in there cooking food for her children, and they leave that tree alone.

I am poor and naked, but I am the chief of the nation. We do not want riches but we do want to train our children right. Riches would do us no good. We could not take them with us to the other world. We do not want riches. We want peace and love.

Red Cloud

Tipi Etiquette

Through research and many lists available, the following seems to be the best listing of etiquette that covers all Native American tribes. The source of the list is unknown and believed to be traditional.

When erecting a tipi, the door should always face East. This is where the Morning Star rises every morning.

If the door is open, a friend may enter the tipi directly. But if it is closed, he should announce his presence and wait for the owner to invite him to come in.

A male enters to the right and waits for the host to invite him to sit to the left of the owner at the rear.

If a woman enters a Tipi, she should enter after the man and must go to the left side. Be hospitable.

Always assume your guest is tired, cold, and hungry.

Always give your guest the place of honor in the lodge and at the feast, and serve him in reasonable ways.

Invited guests are expected to bring their own bowls and spoons.

Never sit while your guests stand.

Women never sit cross-legged like men. They can sit on their heels or with their legs to one side.

If your guests refuse certain foods, say nothing. He may be under vow.

Protect your guest as one of the family.

Do not trouble your guest with many questions about himself. He will tell you what he wants to know.

In another man's lodge, follow his customs-not your own.

Never worry your host with your troubles.

Always repay calls of courtesy. Do not delay.

Give your host a little present upon leaving. Little presents are little courtesies and never offend.

Say "thank you" for every gift, however small.

Compliment, even if you strain the facts to do so. However, it is rude to talk during a meal. Save your compliments for when you are leaving.

Never complement your host's possessions directly, for he then may feel obligated to give the object to you.

Never walk between persons talking.

Never interrupt persons talking.

Always give place to your seniors in entering or leaving the lodge, or anywhere.

Never sit while your seniors stand.

Never force your conversations on anyone.

Speak softly, especially before your elders, or in the presence of strangers.

Younger men remained silent until they were invited to speak.

Never come between anyone and the fire.

Do not stare at strangers. Drop your eyes if they stare hard at you; above all for women.

The women of the lodge are the keepers of the fire, but the men should help with the heavier sticks.

Be kind and generous with those less fortunate.

Show respect to all men and women, but grovel to none.

Let silence be your motto, until duty bids you to speak. Pause to gather your thoughts before speaking. Never speak in haste.

Thank the Great Spirit for every meal.

When the host cleaned his pipe, that was a signal to leave.

When meetings were held by Plains Indians, everyone sat in a circle to indicate harmony and connectedness. A Talking Stick would be passed to the right (clockwise) to indicate the direction the sun travels, and only the person who held the stick could talk. The stick was and still is a symbol of respect for the thoughts and the stories of each member of the circle. All others in the circle were expected to sit quietly and engage in active listening. No one interrupted while the person holding the Talking Stick was speaking. When the person holding the Talking Stick was finished speaking, it was handed to the next person in the circle. If that person chose to not speak, the stick was then handed to the next person until everyone in the circle had participated. Anything could be used as a Talking Stick as long as it had personal meaning.

Grandfather Cries
by Charles Phillip Whitedog

Grandfather, do you know me?
I am your blood.
The son of your son.
I come to ask you a question Grandfather.
Grandfather, don't you know me?
Can I stop being Indian now?
There are others that want to be Indian,
And if they can start from nothing,
I should be able to stop from something?
Grandfather, don't you know me?
Grandfather, I don't look like you.
I don't know what you know.
It would be easy for me to hide behind my paler skin.
No one would know the pain I feel,
Or see the tears I cry for your Great Grandchildren.
Grandfather, don't you know me?
Grandfather, look what I have done to our world.
Mother Earth is on her knees.
The Snake and Owl rule the day.
I don't understand the language you speak Grandfather.
Grandfather, don't you know me?
Grandfather, I want my Pepsi, Levi's and Porsche too.
I want to go where the others go,
And see the things they see too.
I don't have time to dance in the old way Grandfather.
Grandfather?
Grandfather, why are you crying?
Grandfather, why are you crying?
Grandfather, please stop crying.
Grandfather, don't you know me?

The Quill-Work Girl and Her Seven Brothers
A Cheyenne Legend

Hundreds of years ago there was a girl who was very good at quill work, so good that she was the best among all the tribes everywhere. Her designs were radiant with color, and she could decorate anything -- clothing, pouches, quivers, even tipi's.

One day this girl sat down in her parents' lodge and began to make a man's outfit of white buckskin -- war shirt, leggings, moccasins, gauntlets, everything. It took her weeks to embroider them with exquisite quill work and fringes of buffalo hair marvelous to look at. Though her mother said nothing, she wondered. The girl had no brothers, nor was a young man courting her, so why was she making a man's outfit?

As if life wasn't strange enough, no sooner had she finished the first outfit than she began working on a second, then on a third. She worked all year until she had made and decorated seven complete sets of men's clothes, the last a very small one. The mother just watched and kept wondering. At last after the girl had finished the seventh outfit, she spoke to her mother. "Someplace, many days' walk from here, lives seven brothers," she said. "Someday all the world will admire them. Since I am an only child, I want to take them for my brothers, and these clothes are for them."

"It is well, my daughter," her mother said. "I will go with you."

"This is too far for you to walk," said the girl.

"Then I will go part of the way," said her mother.

They loaded their strongest dogs with the seven bundles and set off toward the north. "You seem to know the way," said the mother.

"Yes, I don't know why, but I do," answered the daughter.

"And you seem to know all about these seven young men and what makes them stand out from ordinary humans."

"I know about them," said the girl, "though I don't know how."

Thus they walked, the girl seeming sure of herself. At last the mother said, "This is as far as I can go." They divided the dogs, the girl keeping two for her journey, and took leave of each other. Then the mother headed south back to her village and her husband, while her daughter continued walking into the north.

At last the daughter came to a lone, painted, and very large tipi which stood near a wide stream. The stream was shallow and she waded across it, calling: "It is I, the young-girl-looking-for-brothers, bringing gifts."

At that a small boy about ten years old came out of the tipi. "I am the youngest of seven brothers," he told the girl. "The others are out hunting buffalo, but they'll come back after a while. I have been expecting you. But you'll be a surprise to my brothers, because they don't have my special gifts of `No Touch'."

"What is the gift of no touch?" asked the girl.

"Sometime you'll find out. Well, come into the tipi."

The girl gave the boy the smallest outfit, which fitted him perfectly and delighted him with its beautiful quill work.

"I shall take you all for my brothers," the girl told him.

"And I am glad to have you for a sister," answered the boy.

The girl took all the other bundles off her two dogs' backs and told them to go back to her parents, and at once the dogs began trotting south.

Inside the tipi were seven beds of willow sticks and sage. The girl unpacked her bundles and put a war shirt, a pair of leggings, a pair of moccasins, and a pair of gauntlets upon each of the older brothers' beds. Then she gathered wood and built a fire. From her packs she took dried meat, choke cherries, and kidney fat, and cooked a meal for eight.

Toward evening just as the meal was ready, the six older brothers appeared laden with buffalo meat. The little boy ran outside the lodge and capered, kicking his heels and jumping up and down, showing off his quilled buckskin outfit.

"Where did you get these fine clothes?" the brothers asked.

"We have a new sister," said the child. "She's waiting inside, and she has clothes for you too. She does the most wonderful quill work in the world. And she's beautiful herself!"

The brothers greeted the girl joyfully. They were struck with wonder at the white buckskin outfits she had brought as gifts for them. They were as glad to have a sister to care for as she was to have brothers to cook and make clothes for. Thus they lived happily.

One day after the older brothers had gone out to hunt, a light-colored buffalo- calf appeared at the tipi and scratched and knocked with his hoof against the entrance flap. The boy came out and asked it what it wanted.

"I am sent by the buffalo nation," said the calf. "We have heard of your beautiful sister, and we want her for our own."

"You can't have her," answered the boy. "Go away."

"Oh well, then somebody bigger than I will come," said the calf and ran off jumping and kicking its heels.

The next day when the boy and the sister were alone again, a young heifer arrived, lowing and snorting, rattling the entrance flap of the tipi.

Once more the child came out to ask what she wanted.

"I am sent by the buffalo nation," said the heifer. "We want your beautiful sister for ourselves."

"You can't have her," said the boy. "Go away!"

"Then somebody bigger than I will come," said the heifer, galloping off like the calf before her.

On the third day a large buffalo cow, grunting loudly, appeared at the lodge. The boy came out and asked, "Big buffalo cow, what do you want?"

"I am sent by the buffalo nation," said the cow. "I have come to take your beautiful sister. We want her."

"You can't have her," said the boy. "Go away!"

"Somebody very big will come after me," said the buffalo cow, "and he won't come alone. He'll kill you if you don't give him your sister." With these words the cow trotted off.

On the fourth day the older brothers stayed home to protect the girl. The earth began to tremble a little, then to rock and heave. At last appeared the most gigantic buffalo bull in the world, much larger than any you see now. Behind him came the whole buffalo nation, making the earth shudder. Pawing the ground, the huge bull snorted and bellowed like thunder. The six older brothers, peering out through the entrance hole, were very much afraid, but the little boy stepped boldly outside. "Big, oversized buffalo bull, what do you want from us?" he asked.

"I want your sister," said the giant buffalo bull. "If you won't give her to me, I'll kill you all."

The boy called for his sister and older brothers to come out. Terrified, they did so.

"I'll take her now," growled the huge bull.

"No," said the boy, "she doesn't want to be taken. You can't have her. Go away!"

"In that case I'll kill you now," roared the giant bull. "I'm coming!"

"Quick, brother, use your special medicine!" the six older brothers cried to the youngest.

"I am using it," said he. "Now all of you, catch hold of the branches of this tree. Hurry!" He pointed to a tree growing by the tipi. The girl and the six brothers jumped up into its branches. The boy took his bow and swiftly shot an arrow into the tree's trunk, then clasped the trunk tightly himself. At once the tree started to grow, shooting up into the sky in no time at all. It all happened much, much quicker than it can be told.

The brothers and the girl were lifted up in the tree branches, out of reach of the buffalo. They watched the herd of angry animals grunting and snorting, milling around the tree far below.

"I'll chop the tree down with my horns!" roared the giant buffalo. He charged the tree, which shook like a willow and swayed back and forth. Trying not to fall off, the girl and the brothers clutched the branches. The big bull had gouged a large piece of wood from the trunk.

The little boy said, "I'd better use one more arrow." He shot another arrow high into the treetop, and again the tree grew, shooting up another thousand feet or so, while the seven brothers and the girl rose with it.

The giant buffalo bull made his second charge. Again his horns stabbed into the tree and splintered wood far and wide. The gash in the trunk had become larger.

The boy said, "I must shoot another arrow." He did, hitting the treetop again, and quick as a flash the tree rose another thousand feet.

A third time the bull charged, rocking the tree, making it sway from side to side so that the brothers and the girl almost tumbled out of their branches. They cried to the boy to save them. The child shot a fourth arrow into the tree, which rose again so that the seven young men and the girl disappeared into the clouds. The gash in the tree trunk had become dangerously large.

"When that bull charges again, he will shatter this tree," said the girl. "Little brother, help us!"

Just as the bull charged for the fourth time, the child let loose a single arrow he had left, and the tree rose above the clouds.

"Quick, step out right on the clouds. Hurry!" cried the little boy. "Don't be afraid!"

The bull's head hit the tree trunk with a fearful impact. His horns cut the trunk in two, but just as the tree slowly began to topple, the seven brothers and the girl stepped off its branches and into the sky.

There the eight of them stood. "Little brother, what will become of us now? We can never return to earth; we're up too high. What shall we do?"

"Don't grieve," said the little boy, "I'll turn us into stars."

At once the seven brothers and the girl were bathed in radiant light. They formed themselves into what the white men call the Big Dipper. You can see them there now. The brightest star is the beautiful girl, who is filling the sky with glimmering quill work, and the star twinkling at the very end of the Dipper's handle is the little boy. Can you see him?

Traditional Talking Stick

The Talking Stick is a tool used in many Native American Traditions when a council is called. It allows all council members to present their Sacred Point of View. The Talking Stick is passed from person to person as they speak and only the person holding the stick is allowed to talk during that time period.

The Answering Feather is also held by the person speaking unless the speaker addresses a question to another council member. At that time, the Answering Feather is passed to the person asked to answer the query. Every member of the meeting must listen closely to the words being spoken, so when their turn comes, they do not repeat unneeded information or ask impertinent, questions.

Indian children are taught to listen from age three forward; they are also taught to respect another's viewpoint. This is not to say that they may not disagree, but rather they are bound by their personal honor to allow everyone their Sacred Point of View. People responsible for holding any type council meeting are required to make their own Talking Stick. The Talking Stick may be used when they teach children, hold council, make decisions regarding disputes, hold Pow-Wow gatherings, have storytelling circles, or conduct a ceremony where more than one person will speak.

Since each piece of material used in the Talking Stick speaks of the personal Medicine of the stick owner, each Talking Stick will be different. The Qualities of each type of Standing Person (Tree) brings specific Medicine. White Pine is the Peace Tree, Birch symbolizes truth, Evergreens represent the continued growth of all things. Cedar symbolizes cleansing. Aspen is the symbol for seeing clearly since there are many eye shapes on the truth. Maple represents gentleness. Elm is used for wisdom; Mountain Ash for protection; Oak for strength; Cherry for expression, high emotion, or love. Fruit woods are for abundance and walnut or pecan for gathering of energy or beginning new projects.

Each person making a Talking Stick must decide which type of Standing Person (Tree) will assist their needs and add needed medicine to the Councils held. The ornamentation of each stick all have meaning.

In the Lakotah Tradition, red is for life, yellow is for knowledge, blue is for prayer and wisdom, white is for spirit, purple is for healing, orange is for feeling kinship with all living things, black is for clarity and focus. The type of feathers and hide used on a Talking Stick are very important as well. The Answering Feather is usually an Eagle Feather, which represents high ideals, truth as viewed from the expansive eye of the eagle, and the freedom that comes from speaking total truth to the best of one's ability.

The Answering Feather can also be the feather of a Turkey, the Peace Eagle of the south, which brings peaceful attitudes as well as the give and take necessary in successful completion of disputes.

In the Tribe that see Owl as good Medicine, the Owl feather may also be used to stop deception from entering the Sacred Space of the Council.

The skins, hair or hides used in making a Talking Stick brings the abilities, talents, gifts and medicine of those creatures-beings to council in a variety of ways. Buffalo brings abundance; Elk brings physical fitness and stamina; deer brings gentleness; rabbit brings the ability to listen with big ears; the hair from a horse's tail or mane brings perseverance and adds connection to the earth and to the spirits of the wind.

If an illness of heart, mind, spirit, or body has affected the group gathering, snake skin may be wrapped around the Talking Stick so that healing and transmuting of those poisons can occur. The Talking Stick is the tool that teaches each of us to honor the Sacred Point of View of every living creature.
----Eastern Band of Cherokee Indians ---enrollment # 1009

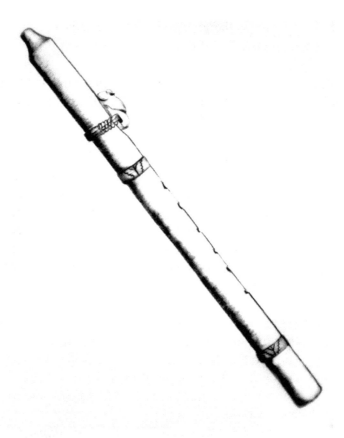

Two Ghostly Lovers

Brule, Sioux

Long ago her lived a young, good-looking man whom no woman could resist. He was an elk charmer--a man who had elk medicine, which carries love power. When this man played the *siyotanka*, the flute, it produced a magic sound. At night a girl hearing it would just get up and go to him, forsaking her father and mother, her own lover, or husband. Maybe her mind told her to stay, but her heart was already beating faster and her feet were running.

Yet the young man, the elk charmer himself, was a lover with a stone heart. He wanted only to conquer women, the way a warrior conquers an enemy. After they came to him once, he had no more use for them. So in spite of his wonderful powers, he did not act as a young man should and was not well liked.

One day when the elk charmer went out to hunt buffalo, he did not return to the village. His parents waited for him day after day, but he never came back. At last they went to a special kind of medicine man who has "finding stones" that give him the power to locate lost things and lost people.

After this holy man had used his finding stones, he told the parents: "I have sad news for you. Your son is dead, and not from sickness or an accident. He was killed. He is lying out there on the prairie."

The medicine man described the spot where they would find the body, it was as he had said. out on the prairie their son was lying dead, stabbed through the heart. Whether he had been killed by an enemy warrior, or a wronged husband from his own tribe, or even a discarded, thrown-away girl, no one ever knew.

His parents dressed him in his finest war shirt, which he had loved more than all his women, and in dead man's moccasins, whose soles are beaded with spirit-land designs. They put his body up on the funeral scaffold, and then the tribe left that part of the country. For it was a very bad thing, this killing which was probably within the tribe. It was, in fact, the very worst thing that could happen, even though everybody was thinking that the young man had brought it on himself.

One evening many days' ride away, when the people had already forgotten this sad happening and were feasting in their tipis, all the dogs in camp started howling. Then the coyotes in the hills took up their mournful cry. Nobody could discover the reason for all this yowling and yipping. But when it finally stopped, the people could hear the hooting of many owls, speaking of death and ghostly things. The laughter in the camp stopped. The fires were put out, and the entry flaps to the tipis were closed.

People tried to sleep, but instead they found themselves listening. They knew a spirit was coming. Finally, they heard the unearthly sounds of a ghost flute and a voice they knew very well--the voice of the dead young man with the elk medicine. They heard this voice singing:

Weeping I roam.
I thought I was the only one
Who had known many loves,
Many girls, many women,
Too many of them.
Now I am having a hard time.
I am roaming, roaming,
And I have to keep roaming
As long as the world stands.

After that night, the people heard the song many times. A lone girl coming home late from a dance, a young woman up before sunrise to get water from the stream, would hear the ghostly song mixed with the sound of the flute. And they would see the shape of a man wrapped in a gray blanket hovering above the ground, for even as a ghost this young man would not leave the girls alone.

Well, it happened long ago, but even now the old-timers at Rosebud, Pine Ridge, and Cheyenne River are still singing this ghost song.

Now, there was another young man who also had a cold heart. He too made love to too many girls and soon threw them away. he was a brave warrior though. He was out a few times with a girl who was in love with him, and he said he would marry her. But he didn't really mean it; he was like many other men who make the same promise only to get under a girl's blanket. One day he said: "I have to go away on a horse stealing raid, I'll be back soon, and then I'll marry you." She told him: "I'll wait for you forever!"

The young warrior went off and never came back; he forgot all about her. The girl, however, waited for a long time.

Well, this young man roamed about for years and had many loves. Then one time when he was hunting, he saw a fine tipi. It had a sun-and-moon design painted on it. He recognized it immediately: it was the tipi of the girl he had left long ago. "Is she still good-looking and loving?" he wondered. "I'll find out!"

He went inside, and there was the girl, lovelier than ever. She was dressed in a white, richly quilled buckskin dress. She smiled at him. "My lover, have you come back at last?"

After serving him a fine meal, she helped him take off his moccasins and his war shirt. She traced his scars from many fights with her fingers. "My warrior," she said, "lie down here beside me, on this soft, soft buffalo robe." He lay down and made love to her, and it was sweeter than he had ever experienced, sweeter than he could have imagined. Then she said: "Rest and sleep now."

The young man--though not very young anymore--woke up in the morning and saw the morning sun shining into the tipi. But the tipi was no longer bright and new; it was ragged and rotting. The buffalo robe under which they had slept was almost hairless and full of holes. He lifted the robe and pulled it aside to look at the girl, and instead of a living, beautiful woman, he found a skeleton. A few strands of black hair still adhered to the skull, which seemed to smile at him. They young girl had died there long ago, waiting for him to come back. He had made love to a spirit. He had embraced bones. He had kissed a skull. He had coupled with a skeleton!

As the thought sank in, the warrior cried aloud, jumped up, and began running in great fear running he knew not where. When he finally came to, he was *witko*, mad. He spoke in strange sounds. His eyes wandered. His thoughts went astray. he was never right in his mind again.

--Told by Lame Deer at Winner Rosebud Indian Reservation, South Dakota, 1970.
Recorded by Richard Erdoes

The Land of the Dead
Serrano

A great hunter brought home a wife. They loved each other and were very happy. But the man's mother hated the young wife, and one day when the husband was out hunting, she put a sharp, pointed object in the wife's seat, and the woman sat down upon it and was killed.

The people immediately brought brush and piled it up. They put her body on it and burned it, and by the time her husband returned that night her body was consumed.

The man went to the burning place and stayed there motionless. Curls of dust rose and whirled about the charred spot. He watched them all night and all day. At evening they grew larger, and at last one larger than all the rest whirled round and round the burned spot. It set off down the road and he set off after it. When it was quite dark, he saw that the dust he was following was his wife, but she would not speak to him.

She was leading him in the direction of the rock past which all dead people go. If they have lived bad lives, the rock falls on them and crushes them. When they came to it, she spoke to her husband. "We are going to the place of dead people," she told him. "I will take you on my back so that you will not be seen and recognized as one of the living."

Thus they traveled on until they came to the river that the dead have to ford. This was very dangerous for the man because he was not dead, but the woman kept him on her back, and they came through safely. The woman went directly to her people, to her parents and brothers and sisters who had died before. They were glad to see her, but they did not like the man, for he was not dead. The woman pleaded for him, however, and they let him stay. Special food always had to be cooked for him, because he could not eat what dead people live on. And in the daytime he could see nothing, it was as if he were alone all day long; only in the night did he see his wife and the other people.

When the dead were going hunting, they took him along and stationed him on the trail the deer would take. Presently he heard them shouting, "The deer, the deer!" and he knew they were shouting to him that the deer were coming in his direction. But he could see nothing. Then he looked again and spotted two little black beetles, which he knocked over. When the people had come up, they praised him for his hunting.

After that the dead did not complain about his presence, but they did feel sorry for him. "It's not time for him to die yet," they said. "He has a hard time here. The woman ought to go back with him." So they arranged for both of them to return, and they instructed the man and the woman to have nothing to do with each other for three nights after they were back on earth.

Three nights for the dead, however, meant three years for the living. Not aware of this, the husband and wife returned to earth and remained continent for three nights. The following evening they embraced, and when the husband woke on the morning of the fourth day, he was alone.

--From a story reported by Ruth Benedict in 1926

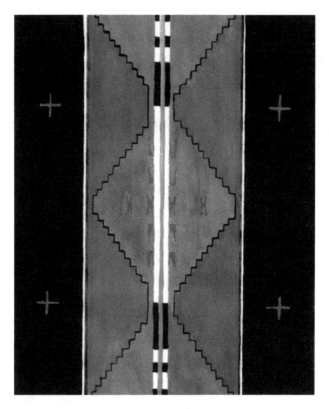

A Cheyenne Blanket

Pawnee

The Cheyennes, like other Indians, do not speak to each other when they are away from the camp. If a man leaves the village and sits or stands by himself on the top of a hill, it is a sign that he wants to be alone, perhaps to meditate, perhaps to pray. No one speaks to him or goes near him.

There was once a Pawnee boy who went off on the warpath to the Cheyenne camp. Somehow he obtained a Cheyenne blanket. He came close to the camp, hid himself and waited. About the middle of the afternoon he left his hiding place and walked to the top of the hill overlooking the village. He had his Cheyenne blanket wrapped about him and over his head, with only a little hole for eyes. He stood quietly watching the camp for an hour or two.

Men began coming in from buffalo hunting, some of them leading packhorses loaded with meat. One hunter was riding a horse packed with meat while he led another packhorse and a black spotted horse that was his running horse. Running horses are ridden only on the chase or on war parties, and after being used they are taken down to the river to be carefully washed and groomed. When the Pawnee boy saw the spotted horse, he knew that his was the one he wanted. The hunter led the animal to his lodge, dismounted and handed the ropes to his women, and went inside.

When the Pawnee made up his mind what he would do. He started down the hill into the village and went straight to the lodge where the women were unloading the meat. Walking up to them, he reached out and took the ropes of the spotted horse and one of the packhorses. The women fell back, doubtless thinking that he was one of the owner's relatives come to take the running horse down to the river. The Pawnee could not speak Cheyenne, but as he turned away he mumbled something, "M-m-m-m-m," in a low voice, and walked toward the river. As soon as he had gone down over the bank and out of sight, he jumped on the spotted horse, rode into the brush, and soon was away with the two animals, stole out of the Cheyenne camp in broad daylight.

--Based on a story collected by George Bird Grinnell in the 1880s

The Gifts of the Little People
An Iroquois Legend

There once was a boy whose parents had died. He lived with his uncle who did not treat him well. The uncle dressed the boy in rags and because of this the boy was called Dirty Clothes.

This boy, Dirty Clothes, was a good hunter. He would spend many hours in the forest hunting food for his lazy uncle who would not hunt for himself.

One day Dirty Clothes walked near the river, with two squirrels that he had shot hanging from his belt. He walked near the cliffs which rose from the water. This is where the

Little People, the Jo-Ge-Oh, often beat their drums. Most of the hunters from the village were afraid to go near this place, but Dirty Clothes remembered the words his mother had spoken years ago, "Whenever you walk with good in your heart, you should never be afraid."

A hickory tree grew there near the river. He saw something moving in its branches. A black squirrel was hopping about high up in the top of the tree. When Dirty Clothes heard a small voice. "Shoot again, Brother," the small voice said. "You still have not hit him."

Dirty Clothes looked down and there near his feet were two small hunters. As he watched, one of them shot an arrow but it fell short of the black squirrel. "Ah," Dirty Clothes thought, "they will never succeed like that. I must help them." He drew his bow and with one shot brought down the squirrel.

The tiny hunters ran to the squirrel. "Whose arrow is this?" asked one of them. They looked up and saw the boy. "Eee-yah," said one of the tiny hunters, "you have shot well. The squirrel is yours."

"Thank you," Dirty Clothes answered, "but the squirrel is yours and also these others I have shot today."

The two small hunters were very glad. "Come with us," they said. "Come visit our lodge so we can thank you properly."

Dirty Clothes thought about his uncle, but it was still early in the day and he could hunt some more after visiting them. "I'll come with you," Dirty Clothes said.

The two Little People led the boy to the river. There a tiny canoe was waiting, only as big as one of his shoes, but his friends told him to step inside. He took one step... and found he had become as small as the tiny hunters and was sitting with them inside their canoe.

The Little People dipped their paddles and up the canoe rose into the air! It flew above the hickory tree, straight to the cliffs and into a cave, the place where the Jo-Ge-Oh people lived. There the two hunters told their story to the other Little People gathered there who greeted the boy as a friend. "You must stay with us." his new friends said, "for just a short time so we can teach you."

Then the Jo-Ge-Oh taught Dirty Clothes things which he had never known. They told him many useful things about the birds and the forest animals. They taught him much about the corn and the squash and the beans which feed human life. They taught him about the strawberries which glow each June like embers in the grass and showed him how to make a special drink which the Little People love.

Last they showed him a new dance to teach his people, a dance to be done in a darkened place so the little People could come and dance with them unseen, a dance which would honor the Jo-Ge-Oh and thank them for their gifts.

Four days passed and the boy knew that the time had come for him to leave. "I must go to my village," he told his friends.

So it was that with the two small hunters he set out walking towards his home. As they walked with him, his two friends pointed to the many plants which were useful and the boy looked at each plant carefully, remembering its name. Later, when he turned to look back at his friends, he found himself standing all alone in a field near the edge of his village.

Dirty Clothes walked into his village wondering how so many things had changed in just four days. It was the same place, yet nothing was the same. People watched him as he walked and finally a woman came up to him. "You are welcome here, Stranger," said the woman. "Please tell us who you are."

"Don't you know?" he answered. 'I am Dirty Clothes."

"How can that be?" said the woman. "Your clothing is so beautiful."

At that, he saw his old rags were gone. The things he wore now were of fine new buckskin, embroidered with moose hair and porcupine quills. "Where is my uncle," he asked the woman, "the one who lived there in that lodge and had a nephew dressed in rags?"

Then an old man spoke up from the crowd. "Ah," said the old man, "that lazy person? He's been dead many years and why would a fine young warrior like you look for such a man?"

Dirty Clothes looked at himself and saw he was no longer a boy. He had become a full-grown man and towered over the people of his village. "I see," he said, "the Little People have given me more gifts than I thought." And he began to tell his story.

The wisest of the old men and women listened well to this young warrior. They learned many things by so listening. That night all his people did the Dark Dance to thank the Jo-Ge-Oh for their gifts and, in the darkness of the lodge, they heard the voices of the Little People joining in the song, glad to know that the human beings were grateful for their gifts. And so it is, even to this day, that the Little People remain the friends of the people of the long-house and the Dark Dance is done, even to this day.

Love is something you and I must have. We must have it because our spirit feeds upon it. We must have it because without it we become weak and faint. Without love our self-esteem weakens. Without it our courage fails. Without love we can no longer look confidently at the world. We turn inward and begin to feed upon our own personalities, and little by little we destroy ourselves. With it we are creative. With it we march tirelessly. With it, and with it alone, we are able to sacrifice for others.

Chief Dan George

Why the Leaves Have Many Colors in Autumn
A Wyandot (Huron) Legend

The wise men turned to him who wrote, then they looked at the trees on many hills. It was the autumn. The leaves had many colors. They said, " We will tell you the story of the battle fought by the deer and the bear in the land of the sky."

The bear was selfish and proud. He often made trouble among the Animals of the Great Council. When he heard that the Deer had walked over the Rainbow Bridge into the sky land he was angry. "I WILL PUNISH THE DEER " he said.

The Bear went to the Rainbow Bridge. He leaped along its beautiful way of glowing colors. He came into the sky land. There he found the deer and said to him; This sky land is the home of the Little Turtle, Why did you come into this land? Why did you not come to meet us in the Great Council? Why did you not wait until all the Animals could come to live here?

Then the Deer was angry, Only the Wolf might ask him such questions. The Bear had no right to speak like that to the Deer.

The Deer said to the Bear, you have gone about making trouble among the Animals long enough You shall never do that again.

The Deer said he would kill the Bear and he arched his neck. He tossed his head to show his long sharp horns. The hair along his back stood up. His eyes blazed as if a fire burned in them. He thought to slay the bear with a single stroke of his terrible horns.

The Bear was not afraid. His claws were very strong. He stood erect for the mighty conflict. His deep growls shook the sky like rolling thunder. The struggle was terrific and long. The Bear was torn by the cruel horns of the Deer.

When the remaining Animals of the great Council heard the awful noise, the Wolf went up into the sky to stop the dreadful battle.

All the animals had to obey the Wolf, so the Deer turned and ran away. And the Bear fled along the paths of the sky. As the Deer ran, the Blood of the Bear dropped from his horns. It fell down to the Lower World and made the leaves of the trees many colors. Some were Red, some Yellow, some were Brown, some Scarlet, and some Crimson.

Now each year when the Autumn comes the leaves of the trees take on these many colors. The forests are flooded with soft and glowing beauty. The Wyandots then say the blood of the Bear has again been thrown down from the sky upon the trees of the Great Island.

Peace and happiness are available in every moment. Peace is every step. We shall walk hand in hand. There are no political solutions to spiritual problems. Remember: If the Creator put it there, it is in the right place. The soul would have no rainbow if the eyes had no tears.

Native American Quote

The Fatal Swing

An Osage Legend
Dorsey, Field Museum:
Anthropological Series, vii,
26, No. 22

Once there was a man living by the big water. He was a deer hunter. He would go out and kill wild turkeys and bring them in. Finally his mother-in-law fell in love with him.

There was a swing by the water, and the old woman and her daughter would swing across it and back. After a while, the old woman partially cut the rope, so that it would break. While the husband was out hunting one day the old woman said to her daughter, "Let us go to the swing, and have some fun."

The old woman got in first, and swung across the water and back. Then the girl got in the swing and she swung across all right, but when she was half-way back, the rope broke in two, and the girl fell into the water and was drowned.

The old woman went home and got supper for her son-in-law. The man came in just at dark, and he missed his wife, and said, "Mother-in-law, where is my wife?" The old woman said, "She has gone to the swing, and has not yet returned." The old woman began to prepare supper for her son-in-law. The man said, "Do not give me any supper."

So he started to cry. The old woman said, "Do not cry; she is dead, and we cannot help it. I will take care of the baby. Your wife got drowned, so she is lost entirely." The man cut off his hair and threw his leggings away and his shirt, and was mourning for his wife. He would go out, and stay a week at a time without eating.

He became very poor. Finally, he said he was going off to stay several days; that he could not help thinking of his wife. He went off and stayed several days, and when he came home he would cry all the time.

One time, when he was out mourning, a rain and thunderstorm came up, and lightning struck all around the tree he was sitting under. He went back home and saw his baby, but stayed out of his sight. Again he went out, and it rained and thundered, and he went up by a big tree and lightning struck a tree near by him.

The Lightning left him a club, and said, "Man, I came here to tell you about your wife for whom you are mourning. You do not know where she is, or how she came to be missing. That old woman drowned her in the big water. The old woman broke the rope and the girl is drowned in the big water. This club you must keep in a safe place. I was sent here to you, and I will help you get your wife back, and you must not be afraid of the big water. Go ahead and try to get her, and the fourth day you will get her all right."

The man went to the big water, and he saw his wife out in the water, and she said, "I cannot get to you. I am tied here with chains. I am going to come up four times." The next time she came out half-way. She said, "Bring me the baby, and I will let her nurse." So the man took the baby to her mother and let her nurse

The woman said, "They are pulling me, and I must go. But the next time you must get me." So she came out the third time up to her knees. The man took the baby to her and let it nurse again. The woman said, "I have got to go back. They are pulling me by the chains. I must go, but the next time will be the last.

I want you to try your best to get me." The man said, "I am going to get you, without doubt." The woman came out the fourth time, and the man hit the chain with the club and it seemed as though lightning struck it, and broke it. He got his wife.

So they went home, and the old woman said, "My daughter, you have got home." But the woman said not a word. Then the man heated an arrow red-hot and put it through the old woman's ears.

So they killed the woman.

The Story of the Peace Pipe

A Sioux Legend
Marie L. McLaughlin, Myths and Legends of the Sioux,
1913

Two young men were out strolling one night talking of love
affairs. They passed around a hill and came to a little ravine
or coulee.

Suddenly they saw coming up from the ravine a beautiful
woman. She was painted and her dress was of the very
finest material.

"What a beautiful girl!" said one of the young men.
"Already I love her. I will steal her and make her my wife."

"No," said the other. "Don't harm her. She may be holy."

The young woman approached and held out a pipe which
she first offered to the sky, then to the earth and then
advanced, holding it out in her extended hands.

"I know what you young men have been saying; one of you
is good, the other is wicked," she said.

She laid down the pipe on the ground and at once became a buffalo cow. The cow pawed the ground, stuck her tail straight out behind her, and then lifted the pipe from the ground again in her hoofs. Immediately she became a young woman again.

"I am come to give you this gift," she said. "It is the peace pipe. Hereafter all treaties and ceremonies shall be performed after smoking it. It shall bring peaceful thoughts into your minds. You shall offer it to the Great Mystery and to mother earth."

The two young men ran to the village and told what they had seen and heard. All the village came out where the young woman was.

She repeated to them what she had already told the young men and added, "When you set free the ghost (the spirit of deceased persons) you must have a white buffalo cow skin."

She gave the pipe to the medicine men of the village, turned again to a buffalo cow and fled away to the land of buffaloes.

Sedna, Mistress of the Underworld

An Eskimo Legend
Boas, Report of the
Bureau of American
Ethnology, vi, 583

Once there lived on a solitary shore an Inung with his daughter Sedna. His wife had been dead for some time and the two led a quiet life.

Sedna grew up to be a handsome girl and the youths came from all around to sue for her hand, but none of them could touch her proud heart. Finally, at the breaking up of the ice in the spring a fulmar flew from over the ice and wooed Sedna with enticing song. "Come to me," it said; "come into the land of the birds, where there is never hunger, where my tent is made of the most beautiful skins. You shall rest on soft bearskins.

My fellows, the fulmars, shall bring you all your heart may desire; their feathers shall clothe you; your lamp shall always be filled with oil, your pot with meat."

Sedna could not long resist such wooing and they went together over the vast sea. When at last they reached the country of the fulmar, after a long and hard journey, Sedna discovered that her spouse had shamefully deceived her. Her new home was not built of beautiful pelts, but was covered with wretched fish-skins, full of holes, that gave free entrance to wind and snow. Instead of soft reindeer skins her bed was made of hard walrus hides and she had to live on miserable fish, which the birds brought her.

Too soon she discovered that she had thrown away her opportunities when in her foolish pride she had rejected the Inuit youth. In her woe she sang: "Aja. O father, if you knew how wretched I am you would come to me and we would hurry away in your boat over the waters. The birds look unkindly upon me the stranger; cold winds roar about my bed; they give me but miserable food. O come and take me back home. Aja."

When a year had passed and the sea was again stirred by warmer winds, the father left his country to visit Sedna. His daughter greeted him joyfully and besought him to take her back home. The father, hearing of the outrages wrought upon his daughter, was determined upon revenge. He killed the fulmar, took Sedna into his boat, and they quickly left the country which had brought so much sorrow to Sedna.

When the other fulmars came home and found their companion dead and his wife gone, they all flew away in search of the fugitives. They were very sad over the death of their poor murdered comrade and continue to mourn and cry until this day.

Having flown a short distance, they discerned the boat and stirred up a heavy storm. The sea rose in immense waves that threatened the pair with destruction. In this mortal peril the father determined to offer Sedna to the birds and flung her overboard. She clung to the edge of the boat with a death grip. The cruel father then took a knife and cut off the first joints of her fingers.

Falling into the sea they were transformed into whales, the nails turning into whalebone.

Sedna holding on to the boat more tightly, the second finger joints fell under the sharp knife and swam away as seals; when the father cut off the stumps of the fingers they became ground seals.

Meantime the storm subsided, for the fulmars thought Sedna was drowned. The father then allowed her to come into the boat again. But from that time she cherished a deadly hatred against him and swore bitter revenge.

After they got ashore, she called her dogs and let them gnaw off the feet and hands of her father while he was asleep.

Upon this he cursed himself, his daughter, and the dogs which had maimed him; whereupon the earth opened and swallowed the hut, the father, the daughter, and the dogs. They have since lived in the land of Adlivun, of which Sedna is the mistress.

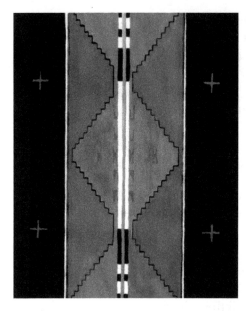

Iktomi's Blanket

A Lakota Legend
Zitkala Sa, Old
Indian Legends,
1901

Alone within his teepee sat Iktomi. The sun was but a hands breadth from the western edge of land. "Those, bad, bad gray wolves! They ate up all my nice fat ducks!" muttered he, rocking his body to and fro. He was cuddling the evil memory he bore those hungry wolves.

At last he ceased to sway his body backward and forward, but sat still and stiff as a stone image. "Oh! I'll go to Inyan, the great-grandfather, and pray for food!" he exclaimed. At once he hurried forth from his teepee and, with his blanket over one shoulder, drew nigh to a huge rock on a hillside. With half-crouching, half-running strides, he fell upon Inyan with outspread hands.

"Grandfather! pity me. I am hungry. I am starving. Give me food. Great-grandfather, give me meat to eat!" he cried. All the while he stroked and caressed the face of the great stone god.

The all-powerful Great Spirit, who makes the trees and grass, can hear the voice of those who pray in many varied ways. The hearing of Inyan, the large hard stone, was the one most sought after. He was the great-grandfather, for he had sat upon the hillside many, many seasons. He had seen the prairie put on a snow-white blanket and then change it for a bright green robe more than a thousand times.

Still unaffected by the myriad moons he rested on the everlasting hill, listening to the prayers of Indian warriors. Before the finding of the magic arrow he had sat there. Now, as Iktomi prayed and wept before the great-grandfather, the sky in the west was red like a glowing face. The sunset poured a soft mellow light upon the huge gray stone and the solitary figure beside it. It was the smile of the Great Spirit upon the grandfather and the wayward child.

The prayer was heard. Iktomi knew it.

"Now, grandfather, accept my offering; 'tis all I have," said Iktomi as he spread his half-worn blanket upon Inyan's cold shoulders. Then Iktomi, happy with the smile of the sunset sky, followed a footpath leading toward a thicketed ravine. He had not gone many paces into the shrubbery when before him lay a freshly wounded deer!

"This is the answer from the red western sky!" cried Iktomi with hands uplifted. Slipping a long thin blade from out his belt, he cut large chunks of choice meat. Sharpening some willow sticks, he planted them around a wood-pile he had ready to kindle. On these stakes he meant to roast the venison.

While he was rubbing briskly two long sticks to start a fire, the sun in the west fell out of the sky below the edge of land. Twilight was over all. Iktomi felt the cold night air upon his bare neck and shoulders. "Ough!" he shivered as he wiped his knife on the grass.

Tucking it in a beaded case hanging from his belt, Iktomi stood erect, looking about. He shivered again.

"Ough! Ah! I am cold. I wish I had my blanket!" whispered he, hovering over the pile of dry sticks and the sharp stakes round about it. Suddenly he paused and dropped his hands at his sides.

"The old great-grandfather does not feel the cold as I do. He does not need my old blanket as I do. I wish I had not given it to him. Oh! I think I'll run up there and take it back!" said he, pointing his long chin toward the large gray stone.

Iktomi, in the warm sunshine, had no need of his blanket, and it had been very easy to part with a thing which he could not miss. But the chilly night wind quite froze his ardent thank-offering. Thus running up the hillside, his teeth chattering all the way, he drew near to Inyan, the sacred symbol.

Seizing one corner of the half-worn blanket, Iktomi pulled it off with a jerk. "Give my blanket back, old grandfather! You do not need it. I do!"

This was very wrong, yet Iktomi did it, for his wit was not wisdom. Drawing the blanket tight over his shoulders, he descended the hill with hurrying feet. He was soon upon the edge of the ravine.

A young moon, like a bright bent bow, climbed up from the southwest horizon a little way into the sky. In this pale light Iktomi stood motionless as a ghost amid the thicket. His woodpile was not yet kindled. His pointed stakes were still bare as he had left them. But where was the deer - the venison he had felt warm in his hands a moment ago?

It was gone.

Only the dry rib bones lay on the ground like giant fingers from an open grave. Iktomi was troubled. At length, stooping over the white dried bones, he took hold of one and shook it. The bones, loose in their sockets, rattled together at his touch. Iktomi let go his hold. He sprang back amazed. And though he wore a blanket his teeth chattered more than ever.

Then his blunted sense will surprise you, reader; for instead of being grieved that he had taken back his blanket, he cried aloud, "Hin-hin-hin! If only I had eaten the venison before going for my blanket!"

Those tears no longer moved the hand of the Generous Giver. They were selfish tears. The Great Spirit does not heed them ever.

Once I was in Victoria, and I saw a very large house.

They told me it was a bank and that the white men place their money there to be taken care of, and that by and by they got it back with interest.

We are Indians and we have no such bank, but when we have plenty of money or blankets, we give them away to other chiefs and people, and by and by they return them with interest, and our hearts feel good.

Our way of giving is our bank.

- Chief Maquinna, Mowachaht (died circa 1795)

A Bashful Courtship

*A Sioux Legend
Marie L.
McLaughlin,
Myths and
Legends of the
Sioux, 1913*

A young man
lived with his
grandmother. He
was a good hunter
and wished to
marry. He knew a
girl who was a
good moccasin
maker, but she
belonged to a great family. He wondered how he could win
her. One day she passed the tent on her way to get water at
the river. His grandmother was at work in the teepee with a
pair of old worn-out sloppy moccasins. The young man
sprang to his feet. "Quick, grandmother! Let me have those
old sloppy moccasins you have on your feet!" he cried.

"My old moccasins, what do you want of them?" cried the
astonished woman.

"Never mind! Quick! I can't stop to talk," answered the
grandson as he caught up the old moccasins the old lady
had doffed, and put them on. He threw a robe over his
shoulders, slipped through the door, and hastened to the
watering place. The girl had just arrived with her bucket.

"Let me fill your bucket for you," said the young man. "Oh,

no, I can do it," the girl said.

"Oh, let me, I can go in the mud. You surely don't want to soil your moccasins," and taking the bucket he slipped in the mud, taking care to push his sloppy old moccasins out so the girl could see them. She giggled outright.

"My, what old moccasins you have!" she cried. "Yes, I have nobody to make me a new pair," he answered. "Why don't you get your grandmother to make you a new pair?" she asked.

"She's old and blind and can't make them any longer. That's why I want you," he answered.

"Oh, you're fooling me. You aren't speaking the truth," she said

"Yes, I am. If you don't believe--come with me now!" said the man.

The girl looked down; so did the youth. At last he said softly, "Well, which is it? Shall I take up your bucket, or will you go with me?"

And she answered, still more softly, "I guess I'll go with you!" The girl's aunt came down to the river, wondering what kept her niece so long. In the mud she found two pairs of moccasin tracks close together; at the edge of the water stood an empty keg.

The Legend of Standing Rock
A Sioux Legend
Marie L. McLaughlin, Myths and Legends of the Sioux, 1913

A Dakota had married an Arikara woman, and by her had one child. By and by he took another wife. The first wife was jealous and pouted. When time came for the village to break camp she refused to move from her place on the tent floor. The tent was taken down, but she sat on the ground with her babe on her back the rest of the camp with her husband went on

At noon her husband halted the line. "Go back to your sister-in-law," he said to his two brothers. "Tell her to come on and we will await you here. But hasten, for I fear she may grow desperate and kill herself."

The two rode off and arrived at their former camping place in the evening. The woman still sat on the ground.

The elder spoke, "Sister-in-law, get up. We have come for you. The camp awaits you."

She did not answer, and he put out his hand and touched her head. She had turned to stone!

The two brothers lashed their ponies and came back to camp. They told their story, but were not believed.

"The woman has killed herself and my brothers will not tell me," said the husband.

However, the whole village broke camp and came back to the place where they had left the woman. Sure enough, she sat there still, a block of stone.

The Indians were greatly excited. They chose out a handsome pony, made a new travois and placed the stone in the carrying net. Pony and travois were both beautifully painted and decorated with streamers and colors.

The stone was thought "wakan" (holy), and was given a place of honor in the center of the camp. Whenever the camp moved the stone and travois were taken along. Thus the stone woman was carried for years, and finally brought to Standing Rock Agency, and now rests upon a brick pedestal in front of the agency office.

From this stone Standing Rock Agency derives its name.

I am a red man. If the Great Spirit had desired me to be a white man he would have made me so in the first place. He put in your heart certain wishes and plans, in my heart he put other and different desires. Each man is good in his sight. It is not necessary for Eagles to be Crows. We are poor... but we are free. No white man controls our footsteps. If we must die... we die defending our rights.

- Sitting Bull, Hunkpapa Lakota (circa 1831-1890)

The Boy and the Turtles

A Sioux Legend
Marie L. McLaughlin,
Myths and Legends of
the Sioux, 1913

A boy went on a turtle hunt, and after following the different streams for hours, finally came to the conclusion that the only place he would find any turtles would be at the little lake, where the tribe always hunted them.

So, leaving the stream he had been following, he cut across country to the lake. On drawing near the lake he crawled on his hands and knees in order not to be seen by the turtles, who were very watchful, as they had been hunted so much.

Peeping over the rock he saw a great many out on the shore sunning themselves, so he very cautiously undressed, so he could leap into the water and catch them before they secreted themselves.

But on pulling off his shirt one of his hands was held up so high that the turtles saw it and jumped into the lake with a great splash.

The boy ran to the shore, but saw only bubbles coming up from the bottom. Directly the boy saw something coming to the surface, and soon it came up into sight. It was a little man, and soon others, by the hundreds, came up and swam about, splashing the water up into the air to a great height.

So scared was the boy that he never stopped to gather up his clothes but ran home naked and fell into his grandmother's tent door.

"What is the trouble, grandchild," cried the old woman.

But the boy could not answer.

"Did you see anything unnatural?"

He shook his head, "no." He made signs to the grandmother that his lungs were pressing so hard against his sides that he could not talk. He kept beating his side with his clenched hands.

The grandmother got out her medicine bag, made a prayer to the Great Spirit to drive out the evil spirit that had entered her grandson's body, and after she had applied the medicine, the prayer must have been heard and answered, as the boy commenced telling her what he had heard and seen.

The grandmother went to the chief's tent and told what her grandson had seen. The chief sent two brave warriors to the lake to ascertain whether it was true or not. The two warriors crept to the little hill close to the lake, and there, sure enough, the lake was swarming with little men swimming about, splashing the water high up into the air. The warriors, too, were scared and hurried home, and in the council called on their return told what they had seen.

The boy was brought to the council and given the seat of honor (opposite the door), and was named "Wankan Wanyanka" (sees holy).

The lake had formerly borne the name of Truth Lake, but from this time on was called "Wicasa-bde"-- Man Lake.

Our land is more valuable than your money.

It will last forever.

It will not even perish by the flames of fire.

As long as the sun shines and the waters flow, this land will be here to give life to men and animals.

Chief Crowfoot, Siksika (circa 1825-1890)

The Simpleton's Wisdom

*A Sioux Legend
Marie L.
McLaughlin, Myths
and Legends of the
Sioux, 1913*

There was a man and his wife who had one daughter. Mother and daughter were deeply attached to one another, and when the latter died the mother was disconsolate.

She cut off her hair, cut gashes in her cheeks and sat before the corpse with her robe drawn over her head, mourning for her dead. She would not let them touch the body to take it to a burying scaffold.

She had a knife in her hand, and if anyone offered to come near the body the mother would wail, "I am weary of life. I do not care to live. I will stab myself with this knife and join my daughter in the land of spirits."

Her husband and relatives tried to get the knife from her, but could not. They feared to use force lest she kill herself. They came together to see what they could do.

"We must get the knife away from her," they said.

At last they called a boy, a kind of simpleton, yet with a good deal of natural shrewdness. He was an orphan and very poor. His moccasins were out at the sole and he was dressed in wei-zi (coarse buffalo skin, smoked).

"Go to the teepee of the mourning mother, " they told the simpleton, "and in some way contrive to make her laugh and forget her grief. Then try to get the knife away from her."

The boy went to the tent and sat down at the door as if waiting to be given something. The corpse lay in the place of honor where the dead girl had slept in life. The body was wrapped in a rich robe and wrapped about with ropes.

Friends had covered it with rich offerings out of respect to the dead.

As the mother sat on the ground with her head covered she did not at first see the boy, who sat silent. But when his reserve had worn away a little he began at first lightly, then more heavily, to drum on the floor with his hands.

After a while he began to sing a comic song. Louder and louder he sang until carried away with his own singing he sprang up and began to dance, at the same time gesturing and making all manner of contortions with his body, still singing the comic song. As he approached the corpse he waved his hands over it in blessing.

The mother put her head out of the blanket and when she saw the poor simpleton with his strange grimaces trying to do honor to the corpse by his solemn waving, and at the same time keeping up his comic song, she burst out laughing. Then she reached over and handed her knife to the simpleton.

"Take this knife," she said. "You have taught me to forget my grief. If while I mourn for the dead I can still be mirthful, there is no reason for me to despair. I no longer care to die. I will live for my husband."

The simpleton left the teepee and brought the knife to the astonished husband and relatives.

"How did you get it? Did you force it away from her, or did you steal it?" they asked.

"She gave it to me. How could I force it from her or steal it when she held it in her hand, blade uppermost? I sang and danced for her and she burst out laughing. Then she gave it to me," he answered.

When the old men of the village heard the orphan's story they were very silent. It was a strange thing for a lad to dance in a teepee where there was mourning. It was stranger that a mother should laugh in a teepee before the corpse of her dead daughter.

The old men gathered at last in a council. They sat a long time without saying anything, for they did not want to decide hastily. The pipe was filled and passed many times. At last an old man spoke.

"We have a hard question. A mother has laughed before the

corpse of her daughter, and many think she has done foolishly, but I think the woman did wisely. The lad was simple and of no training, and we cannot expect him to know how to do as well as one with good home and parents to teach him. Besides, he did the best that he knew. He danced to make the mother forget her grief, and he tried to honor the corpse by waving over it his hands."

"The mother did right to laugh, for when one does try to do us good, even if what he does causes us discomfort, we should always remember rather the motive than the deed. And besides, the simpleton's dancing saved the woman's life, for she gave up her knife. In this, too, she did well, for it is always better to live for the living than to die for the dead."

Honor the sacred.
Honor the Earth, our Mother.
Honor the Elders.
Honor all with whom we
share the Earth:-
Four-leggeds, two-leggeds,
winged ones,
Swimmers, crawlers,
plant and rock people.
Walk in balance and beauty.

Native American Elder

The Skin Shifting Old Woman

A Wichita Legend Dorsey, Publications of the Carnegie Institution, xxi, 124, No. 17

In the story of Healthy-Flint-Stone-Man, it is told that he was a powerful man and lived in a village and was a chief of the place. He was not a man of heavy build, but was slim.

Often when a man is of this type of build he is called "Healthy-Flint-Stone-Man," after the man in the story. Healthy-Flint-Stone-Man had parents, but at this time he had no wife. Soon afterwards he married, and his wife was the prettiest woman that ever lived in the village. When she married Healthy-Flint-Stone-Man they lived at his home.

She was liked by his parents, for she was a good worker and kind-hearted. As was their custom, the men of the village came at night to visit Healthy-Flint-Stone-Man, and his wife did the cooking to feed them, so that he liked her all the more, and was kind to her.

Early in the morning a strange woman by the name of Little-Old-Woman came to their place and asked the wife to go with her to get wood. Out of kindness to Little-Old-Woman she went with her, leaving her husband at home. Little-Old-Woman knew where all the dry wood was to be found. When they reached the place where she thought there was plenty of wood they did not stop.

They went on past, although there was plenty of good dry wood. The wife began to cut wood for the old woman and some for herself. When she had cut enough for both she fixed it into two bundles, one for each. Little-Old-Woman knelt by her pile and waited for the wife to help her up. Little-Old-Woman then helped the wife in the same way, and they started toward their home. They talked on the way about their manner of life at home. Arrived at the village, the old woman went to her home. When the wife got home she began to do her work.

Again, the second time, the old woman came around and asked the wife to go with her to fetch wood. They started away together, and this time went farther than on the first time to get their wood, though they passed much good wood. The wife cut wood for both and arranged it in two piles, but this time she herself first knelt by her pile and asked the old woman to take hold of her hands and pull her up; then the wife helped the old woman with her load.

They returned home, and on the way the old woman said to the wife, "If you will go with me to fetch wood for the fourth time I shall need no more help from you." They again went far beyond where any other women had gone to get wood. When they got to the village they parted. The wife wondered why the old woman came to her for help. She found the men passing the time talking of the past as usual. She kept on doing her duty day after day.

The third time the old woman came for the wife to ask her to help her fetch wood, as she was all out of it again. Again they went out, and this time they went still further for the wood, and now they were getting a long way from the village. The wife cut wood and arranged it in two bundles, one for each of them to carry. This time it was the old woman's turn first to be helped up with the wood.

They helped each other, and on the way home the old woman told the wife that they had only once more to go for wood, and the work would all be done. She always seemed thankful for the help she received. They reached the village and went to their homes. The wife found her men as usual, and commenced to do her work. After the men were through eating they went home, though some stayed late in the night.

Finally, the old woman came the fourth time to ask the wife to go with her and help her fetch some wood. This time they went about twice as far as they had gone the third time from the village. When the old woman thought they were far enough they stopped, and the wife began cutting wood for both of them. When she had cut enough she arranged it in two bundles. Now it was the wife's turn to be helped up with the wood, but the old woman refused to do it as usual and told her to go ahead and kneel by the bundle of wood. The wife refused.

Now, each tried to persuade the other to kneel first against the bundle of wood. The old woman finally prevailed, and the wife knelt against the wood, and as she put her robe around her neck the old woman seemed pleased to help her, but as the old woman was fixing the carrying ropes she tightened them, after slipping them around the wife's neck until the wife fell at full length, as though dying.

The old woman sat down to rest, as she was tired from choking the wife. Soon she got up and untied the wife. Now, they were in the thick timber, and there was flowing water through it. After the old woman had killed the wife she blew into the top of her head and blew the skin from her, hair and all. This she did because she envied the wife her good looks, since the wife was the best-looking woman in the village, and her husband was good-looking and well thought of by all the prominent men, and the old woman wanted to be treated as well as the wife had been treated.

Then the old woman began to put on the wife's skin, but the wife was a little smaller than the old woman, though the old woman managed to stretch the skin and drew it over her, fitting herself to it. Then she smoothed down the skin until it fitted her nicely. She took the wife's body to the flowing water and threw it in, having found a place that was never visited by anyone, and that had no trail leading to it. She then went to her pile of wood and took it to her home. She found the men visiting the chief.

The chief did not discover that she was not his wife. The old woman knew all about the former wife's ways, for she had talked much with her when they were coming home with the wood, and she had asked the wife all sorts of questions about her husband. She understood how the men carried on at the chief's place. The wife had told the chief that the old woman had said that they were to go for wood four different times, and the last time being the fourth time, he supposed it was all over and his wife had got through with the old woman. So, as the old woman was doing his wife's duty, he thought her to be his wife until the time came when the skin began to decay and the hair to come off. Still there were big crowds of men around, and the old woman began to be fearful lest they would find her out. So she made as if she were sick. The chief tried to get a man to doctor her, but she refused to be doctored. Finally, he hired a servant to doctor her. This was the man who always sat right by the entrance, ready to do errands or carry announcements to the people. His name was Buffalo-

Crow-Man. He had a dark complexion. The old woman began to rave at his medicine working.

He began to tell who the old woman was, saying that there was no need of doctoring her; that she was a fraud and an evil spirit; and that she had become the wife of the chief through her bad deeds. The old woman told the chief not to believe the servant; and that he himself was a fraud and was trying to get her to do something wrong. The servant then stood at the feet of the old woman and began to sing.

Then over her body he went and jumped at her head. Then he commenced to sing again, first on her left side, then on her right. He sang the song four times, and while he was doing this the decayed hide came off from her. The servant told the men to take her out and take her life for what she had done to the chief's wife, telling how she had fooled the chief. They did as they were told.

The servant told the men he had suspected the old woman when she had come around to get the wife to go after wood with her; that when going after wood they always went a long distance, so that no one could observe them, but that he had always flown very high over them, so they could not see him, and had watched them; that on the fourth time they went for wood he had seen the old woman choke the wife with the wife's rope; how the old woman had secured the whole skin of the wife and had thrown her body into the flowing water. He told the men where the place was, and directed them there the next day. The men went to their homes, feeling very sad for the wicked thing the old woman had done.

On the next day the chief went as directed, and he came to a place where he found a pile of wood that belonged to his former wife. He went to the place where he supposed his wife to be. He sat down and commenced to weep. There he stayed all night and the next day. He returned to his home, but he could not forget the occurrence. So he went back again and stayed another night and again returned home.

The chief was full of sorrow. He went back to the place the third time, and when he got there he sat down and commenced to weep. Again he stayed all night, and early next morning it was foggy and he could not see far. While he sat and wept he faced the east, and he was on the west side of the flowing waters, so that he also faced the flowing water wherein his wife's body was thrown.

He heard some one singing, but he was unable to catch the sound so that he could locate the place where the sound came from. He finally discovered that it came from the flowing water. He went toward the place and listened, and indeed it was his wife's voice, and this is what she sang:

Woman-having-Powers-in-the-Water, Woman-having-Powers-in-the-Water, I am the one (you seek), I am here in the water.

As he went near the river he saw in the middle of the water his wife standing on the water. She told him to go back home and tell his parents to clean their grass-lodge and to purify the room by burning sage. She told her husband that he might then return and take her home; that he should tell his parents not to weep when she should return, but that they should rejoice at her return to life, and that after that he could take her home. So the man started to his home.

After he arrived he told his mother to clean and purify the lodge; and that he had found his wife and that he was going back again to get her. He told her that neither she nor any of their friends should weep at sight of the woman. While his mother was doing this cleaning he went back to the river and stayed one more night, and early in the morning he heard the woman singing again. He knew that he was to bring his wife back to his home. When he heard her sing he went straight to her.

She came out of the water and he met her. She began to tell her husband about her troubles--how she met troubles and how he was deceived. That day they went to their home, and Flint-Stone-Man's parents were glad to see his wife back once more. They lived together until long afterward.

The beauty of the trees,
the softness of the air,
the fragrance of the grass,
speaks to me.

The summit of the mountain,
the thunder of the sky,
the rhythm of the sea,
speaks to me.

The strength of the fire,
the taste of salmon,
the trail of the sun,
and the life that never goes away,
they speak to me.

And my heart soars.

- Chief Dan George, Tsleil-Waututh (1899 - 1981)

The Foster Child of the Deer

A Zuni Legend
Frank Hamilton Cushing, Zuni Folk Tales, 1901

Once, long, long ago, at Háwikuh, there lived a maiden most beautiful. In her earlier years her father, who was a great priest, had devoted her to sacred things, and kept her always in the house secure from the gaze of all men, and thus she grew.

She was so beautiful that when the Sun looked down along one of the straight beams of his own light, if one of those beams chanced to pass through a chink in the roof, the skyhole, or the windows of the upper part of the maiden's room, he beheld her and wondered at her rare beauty, unable to compare it with anything he saw in his great journeys round about the worlds.

Thus, as the maiden grew apace and became a young woman, the Sun loved her exceedingly, and as time went on he became so enamored of her that he descended to earth and entered on one of his own beams of light into her apartment, so that suddenly, while she was sitting one noon-day weaving pretty baskets, there stood before her a glorious youth, gloriously dressed.

It was the Sun-father. He looked upon her gently and lovingly; she looked upon him not fearfully: and so it came about that she loved him and he loved her, and he won her to be his wife. And many were the days in which he visited her and dwelt with her for a space at noon-time; but as she was alone mostly, or as she kept sitting weaving her trays when any one of the family entered her apartment, no one suspected this.

Now, as she knew that she had been devoted to sacred things, and that if she explained how it was that she was a mother she would not be believed, she was greatly exercised in mind and heart. She therefore decided that when her child was born she would put it away from her.

When the time came, the child one night was born. She carefully wrapped the little baby boy in some soft cotton-wool, and in the middle of the night stole out softly over the rooftops, and, silently descending, laid the child on the sheltered side of a heap of refuse near the little stream that flows by Háwikuh, in the valley below. Then, mourning as a mother will mourn for her offspring, she returned to her room and lay herself down, poor thing, to rest.

As daylight was breaking in the east, and the hills and the valleys were coming forth one after another from the shadows of night, a Deer with her two little brightly-speckled fawns descended from the hills to the south across the valley, with ears and eyes alert, and stopped at the stream to drink.

While drinking they were startled by an infant's cry, and, looking up, they saw dust and cotton-wool and other things flying about in the air, almost as if a little whirlwind were blowing on the site of the refuse-heap where the child had been laid. It was the child, who, waking and finding itself alone, hungry, and cold, was crying and throwing its little hands about. "Bless my delight!" cried the Deer to her fawns. I have this day found a waif, a child, and though it be human it shall be mine; for, see, my children, I love you so much that surely I could love another."

Thereupon she approached the little infant, and breathed her warm breath upon it and caressed it until it became quiet, and then after wrapping about it the cotton-wool, she gently lifted it on her broad horns, and, turning, carried it steadily away toward the south, followed on either side by her children, who kept crying out "Neh! neh!" in their delight.

The home of this old Deer and her little ones, where all her children had been born for years, was south of Háwikuh, in the valley that turns off among the ledges of rocks near the little spring called Póshaan. There, in the shelter of a clump of piñon and cedar trees, was a soft and warm retreat, winter and summer, and this was the lair of the Deer and her young.

The Deer was no less delighted than surprised next morning to find that the infant had grown apace, for she had suckled it with her own milk, and that before the declining of the sun it was already creeping about. And greater was her surprise and delight, as day succeeded day, to find that the child grew even more swiftly than grow the children of the Deer. Behold! on the evening of the fourth day it was running about and playing with its foster brother and sister. Nor was it slow of foot, even as compared with those little Deer.

Behold! yet greater cause for wonder, on the eighth day it was a youth fair to look upon-looking upon itself and seeing that it had no clothing, and wondering why it was not clothed, like its brother and sister, in soft warm hair with pretty spots upon it.

As time went on, this little foster-child of the Deer (it must always be remembered that it was the offspring of the Sun-father himself), in playing with his brother and sister, and in his runnings about, grew wondrously strong, and even swifter of foot than the Deer themselves, and learned the language of the Deer and all their ways.

When he had become perfected in all that a Deer should know, the Deer-mother led him forth into the wilds and made him acquainted with the great herd to which she belonged. They were exceedingly happy with this addition to their number; much they loved him, and so sagacious was the youth that he soon became the leader of the Deer of the Háwikuh country.

When these Deer and the Antelopes were out on the mesas ranging to and fro, there at their head ran the swift youth. The soles of his feet became as hard as the hoofs of the Deer, the skin of his person strong and dark, the hair of his head long and waving and as soft as the hair on the sides of the Deer themselves.

It chanced one morning, late that summer, that the uncle of the maiden who had cast away her child went out hunting, and he took his way southward past Póshaan, the lair of the Deer-mother and her foster-child. As he traversed the borders of the great mesas that lie beyond, he saw a vast herd of Deer gathered, as people gather in council. They were quiet and seemed to be listening intently to some one in their midst.

The hunter stole along carefully on hands and knees, twisting himself among the bushes until he came nearer; and what was his wonder when he beheld, in the midst of the Deer, a splendid youth, broad of shoulder, tall and strong of limb, sitting nude and graceful on the ground, and the old Deer and the young seemed to be paying attention to what he was saying.

The hunter rubbed his eyes and looked again; and again he looked, shading his eyes with his hands. Then he elevated himself to peer yet more closely, and the sharp eyes of the youth discovered him. With a shout he lifted himself to his feet and sped away like the wind, followed by the whole herd, their hoofs thundering, and soon they were all out of sight.

The hunter dropped his bow and stood there musing; then picking it up, he turned himself about and ran toward Háwikuh as fast as he could. When he arrived he related to the father of the girl what he had seen. The old priest summoned his hunters and warriors and bade the uncle repeat the story. Many there were who said: "You have seen an apparition, and of evil omen to your family, alas! alas!"

"No," said he, "I looked, and again I looked, and yet again, and again, and I avow to you that what I saw was as plain and as mortal as the Deer themselves."

Convinced at last, the council decided to form a grand hunt, and word was given from the housetops that on the fourth day from that day a hunt should be undertaken--that the southern mesa should be surrounded, and that the people should gather in from all sides and encompass the herd there, in order that this wonderful youth should not escape being seen, or possibly captured.

Now, when the Deer had gone to a safe distance they slackened their pace and called to their leader not to fear. And the old foster-mother of the youth for the first time related to him, as she had related to them long ago, that he was the child of mortals, telling how she had found him.

The youth sat with his head bowed, thinking of these

things. Then he raised his head proudly, and said: "What though I be the child of mortals, they have not loved me: they have cast me from their midst, therefore will I be faithful to thee alone."

But the old Deer-mother said to him: "Hush, my child! Thou art but a mortal, and though thou might'st live on the roots of the trees and the bushes and plants that mature in autumn, yet surely in the winter time thou could'st not live, for my supply of milk will be withholden, and the fruits and the nuts will all be gone."

And the older members of that large herd gathered round and repeated what she had been saying. And they said: "We are aware that we shall be hunted now, as is the invariable custom when our herd has been discovered, on the fourth day from the day on which we were first seen. Amongst the people who come there will be, no doubt, those who will seek you; and you must not endeavor to escape.

Even we ourselves are accustomed to give up our lives to the brave hunters among this people, for many of them are sacred of thought, sacred of heart, and make due sacrifices unto us, that our lives in other form may be spared unceasingly."

A splendid Deer rose from the midst of the herd, and, coming forward, laid his cheek on the cheek of the boy, and said: "Yet we love you, but we must now part from you. And, in order that you may be like unto other mortals, only exceeding them, accompany me to the Land of the Souls of Men, where sit in council the Gods of the Sacred Dance and Drama, the Gods of the Spirit World."

To all this the youth, being convinced, agreed. And on that same day the Deer who had spoken set forward, the swift youth running by his side, toward the Lake of the Dead. On and on they sped, and as night was falling they came to the borders of that lake, and the lights were shining over its middle and the Gardens of the Sacred Dance. And the old Drama-woman and the old Drama-man were walking on its shores, back and forth, calling across to each other.

As the Deer neared the shore of the lake, he turned and said to his companion: "Step in boldly with me. Ladders of rushes will rise to receive you, and down underneath the waters into the great Halls of the Dead and of the Sacred Dance we will be borne gently and swiftly."

Then they stepped into the lake. Brighter and lighter it grew. Great ladders of rushes and flags lifted themselves from the water, and upon them the Deer and his companion were borne downward into halls of splendor, lighted by many lights and fires.

And in the largest chamber the gods were sitting in council silently. Páutiwa, the Sun-priest of the Sacred Drama (Kâkâ), Shúlawitsi (the God of Fire), with his torch of ever-living flame, and many others were there; and when the strangers arrived they greeted and were greeted, and were given a place in the light of the central fire.

And in through the doors of the west and the north and the east and the south filed long rows of sacred dancers, those who had passed through the Lake of the Dead, clad in cotton mantles, white as the daylight, finely embroidered, decked with many a treasure shell and turquoise stone. These performed their sacred rites, to the delight of the gods and the wonder of the Deer and his foster-brother.

And when the dancers had retired, Páutiwa, the Sun-priest of the Sacred Dance, arose, and said: "What would'st thou?"-though he knew full well beforehand. "What would'st thou, oh, Deer of the forest mesas, with thy companion, thy foster-brother; for not thinking of nothing would one visit the home of the Kâkâ."

Then the Deer lifted his head and told his story.

"It is well," said the gods.

"Appear, my faithful one," said Páutiwa to Shúlawitsi. And Shúlawitsi appeared and waved his flame around the youth, so that he became convinced of his mortal origin and of his dependence upon food prepared by fire. Then the gods who speak the speech of men gathered around and breathed upon the youth, and touched to his lips moisture from their own mouths, and touched the portals of his ears with oil from their own ears, and thus was the youth made acquainted with both the speech and the understanding of the speech of mortal man.

Then the gods called out, and there were brought before them fine garments of white cotton embroidered in many colors, rare necklaces of sacred shell with many turquoises and coral-like stones and shells strung in their midst, and all that the most beautifully clad of our ancients could have glorified their appearance with. Such things they brought forth, and, making them into a bundle, laid them at the feet of the youth.

Then they said: "Oh, youth, oh, brother and father, since thou art the child of the Sun, who is the father of us all, go forth with thy foster-brother to thy last meeting-place with him and with his people; and when on the day after the morrow hunters shall gather from around thy country, some of ye, oh, Deer," said he, turning to the Deer, "'yield thyselves up that ye may die as must thy kind ever continue to die, for the sake of this thy brother."

"I will lead them," simply replied the Deer.

"Thanks."

And Páutiwa continued: "Here full soon wilt thou be gathered in our midst, or with the winds and the mists of the air at night-time wilt sport, ever-living. Go ye forth, then, carrying this bundle, and, as ye best know how, prepare this our father and child for his reception among men. And, O son and father," continued the priest-god, turning to the youth, "Fear not! Happy wilt thou be in the days to come, and treasured among men.

Hence thy birth. Return with the Deer and do as thou art told to do. Thy uncle, leading his priest-youths, will be foremost in the hunt. He will pursue thee and thy foster-mother. Lead him far away; and when thou hast so led him, cease running and turn and wait, and peacefully go home whither he guides thee."

The sounds of the Sacred Dance came in from the outer apartments, and the youth and the Deer, taking their bundle, departed. More quickly than they had come they sped away; and on the morning when the hunters of Háwikuh were setting forth, the Deer gathered themselves in a vast herd on the southern mesa, and they circled about the youth and instructed him how to unloose the bundle he had brought.

Then closer and closer came the Deer to the youth and bade him stand in his nakedness, and they ran swiftly about him, breathing fierce, moist breaths until hot steam enveloped him and bathed him from head to foot, so that he was purified, and his skin was softened, and his hair hung down in a smooth yet waving mass at the back of his head.

Then the youth put on the costume, one article after another, he having seen them worn by the Gods of the Sacred Dance, and by the dancers; and into his hair at the back, under the band which he placed round his temples, he thrust the glowing feathers of the macaw which had been given him. Then, seeing that there was still one article left, --a little string of conical shells, --he asked what that was for; and the Deer told him to tie it about his knee.

The Deer gathered around him once more, and the old chief said: "Who among ye are willing to die?" And, as if it were a festive occasion to which they were going, many a fine Deer bounded forth, striving for the place of those who were to die, until a large number were gathered, fearless and ready. Then the Deer began to move.

Soon there was an alarm. In the north and the west and the south and the east there was cause for alarm. And the Deer began to scatter, and then to assemble and scatter again. At last the hunters with drawn bows came running in, and soon their arrows were flying in the midst of those who were devoted, and Deer after Deer fell, pierced to the heart or other vital part.

At last but few were left, --amongst them the kind old Deer-mother and her two children; and, taking the lead, the glorious youth, although encumbered by his new dress, sped forth with them. They ran and ran, the fleetest of the tribe of Háwikuh pursuing them; but all save the uncle and his brave sons were soon left far behind. The youth's foster-brother was soon slain, and the youth, growing angry, turned about; then bethinking himself of the words of the gods, he sped away again. So his foster-sister, too, was killed; but he kept on, his old mother alone running behind him.

At last the uncle and his sons overtook the old mother, and they merely caught her and turned her away, saying: "Faithful to the last she has been to this youth." Then they renewed the chase for the youth; and he at last, pretending weariness, faced about and stood like a stag at bay. As soon as they approached, he dropped his arms and lowered his head. Then he said: "Oh, my uncle" (for the gods had told who would find him) --" Oh, my uncle, what wouldst thou? Thou hast killed my brothers and sisters; what wouldst thou with me?

The old man stopped and gazed at the youth in wonder and admiration of his fine appearance and beautiful apparel. Then he said: "Why dost thou call me uncle?"

"Because, verily," replied the youth, "thou art my uncle, and thy niece, my maiden-mother, gave birth to me and cast me away upon a dust-heap; and then my noble Deer found me and nourished me and cherished me."

The uncle and his sons gazed still with wonder. Then they thought they saw in the youth's clear eyes and his soft, oval face a likeness to the mother, and they said: "Verily, this which he says is true." Then they turned about and took him by the hands gently and led him toward Háwikuh, while one of them sped forward to test the truth of his utterances.

When the messenger arrived at Háwikuh he took his way straight to the house of the priest, and told him what he had heard. The priest in anger summoned the maiden.

"Oh, my child," said he, "hast thou done this thing which we are told thou hast done?" And he related what he had been told.

"Nay, no such thing have I done," said she.

"Yea, but thou hast, oh, unnatural mother! And who was the father?" demanded the old priest with great severity.

Then the maiden, thinking of her Sun-lover, bowed her head in her lap and rocked herself to and fro, and cried sorely. And then she said: "Yea, it is true; so true that I feared thy Wrath, oh, my father! I feared thy shame, oh, my mother! and what could I do?" Then she told of her lover, the Sun, --with tears she told it, and she cried out: "Bring back my child that I may nurse him and love but him alone, and see him the father of children!"

By this time the hunters arrived, some bringing game, but others bringing in their midst this wondrous youth, on whom each man and maiden in Háwikuh gazed with delight and admiration.

They took him to the home of his priest-grandfather; and as though he knew the way he entered the apartment of his mother, and she, rising and opening wide her arms, threw herself on his breast and cried and cried. And he laid his hand on her head, and said: "Oh, mother, weep not, for I have come to thee, and I will cherish thee.

So was the foster-child of the Deer restored to his mother and his people.

Wondrously wise in the ways of the Deer and their language was he--so much so that, seeing them, he understood them. This youth made little ado of hunting, for he knew that he could pay those rites and attentions to the Deer that were most acceptable, and made them glad of death at the hand of the hunter. And ere long, so great was his knowledge and success, and his preciousness in the eyes of the Master of Life, that by his will and his arm alone the tribe of Háwikuh was fed and was clad in buckskins.

A rare and beautiful maiden he married, and most happy was he with her.

It was his custom to go forth early in the morning, when the Deer came down to drink or stretch themselves and walk abroad and crop the grass; and, taking his bow and quiver of arrows, he would go to a distant mesa, and, calling the Deer around him, and following them as swiftly as they ran, he would strike them down in great numbers, and, returning, say to his people: "Go and bring in my game, giving me only parts of what I have slain and taking the rest yourselves."

So you can readily see how he and his people became the greatest people of Háwikuh. Nor is it marvelous that the sorcerers of that tribe should have grown envious of his prosperity, and sought to diminish it in many ways, wherein they failed.

At last one night the Master of Sorcerers in secret places raised his voice and cried "Weh-h-h-h! Weh-h-h-h-h-h!" And round about him presently gathered all the sorcerers of the place, and they entered into a deep cavern, large and lighted by green, glowing fires, and there, staring at each other, they devised means to destroy this splendid youth, the child of the Sun.

One of their number stood forth and said: "I will destroy him in his own vocation. He is a hunter, and the Coyote loves well to follow the hunter." His words were received with acclamation, and the youth who had offered himself sped forth in the night to prepare, by incantation and with his infernal appliances, a disguise for himself.

On the next morning, when the youth went forth to hunt, an old Coyote sneaked behind him after he reached the mesas, and, following stealthily, waited his throwing down of the Deer; and when the youth had called and killed a number of Deer and sat down to rest on a fallen tree, the Coyote sneaked into sight. The youth, looking at him, merely thought: "He seeks the blood of my slain Deer," and he went on with his prayers and sacrifices to the dead of the Deer. But soon, stiffening his limbs, the Coyote swiftly scudded across the open, and, with a puff from his mouth and nostrils like a sneeze toward the youth, threw himself against him and arose a man, --the same man who had offered his services in the council of the wizards--while the poor youth, falling over, ran away, a human being still in heart and mind, but in form a coyote.

Off to the southward he wandered, his tail dragging in the dust; and growing hungry he had naught to eat; and cold on the sides of the mesas he passed the night, and on the following morning wandered still, until at last, very hungry, he was fain even to nip the blades of grass and eat the berries of the juniper. Thus he became ill and worn; and one night as he was seeking a warm place to lay him down and die, he saw a little red light glowing from the top of a hillock. Toward this light he took his way, and when he came near he saw that it was shining up through the sky hole of someone's house. He peered over the edge and saw an old Badger with his grizzly wife, sitting before a fire, not in the form of a badger but in the form of a little man, his badger-skin hanging beside him. Then the youth raid to himself I will cast myself down into their house, thus showing them my miserable condition." And as he tried to step down the ladder, he fell, teng, on the floor before them.

The Badgers were disgusted. They grabbed the Coyote, and hauling him up the ladder, threw him into the plain, where, toonoo, he fell far away and swooned from loss of breath. When he recovered his thoughts he again turned toward the glowing skyhole, and, crawling feebly back, threw himself down into the room again. Again he was thrown out, but this time the Badger said: "It is marvelously strange that this Coyote, the miserable fellow, should insist on coming back, and coming back."

"I have heard," said the little old Badger-woman, "that our glorious beloved youth of Háwikuh was changed some time ago into a Coyote. It may be he. Let us see when he comes again if it be he. For the love of mercy, let us see!"

Ere long the youth again tried to clamber down the ladder, and fell with a thud on the floor before them. A long time he lay there senseless, but at last opened his eyes and looked about. The Badgers eagerly asked if he were the same who had been changed into a Coyote, or condemned to inhabit the form of one. The youth could only move his head in acquiescence.

Then the Badgers hastily gathered an emetic and set it to boil, and when ready they poured the fluid down the throat of the seeming Coyote, and tenderly held him and pitied him. Then they laid him before the fire to warm him. Then the old Badger, looking about in some of his burrows, found a sacred rock crystal, and heating it to glowing heat in the fire, he seared the palms of the youth's hands, the soles of his feet, and the crown of his head, repeating incantations as he performed this last operation, whereupon the skin burst and fell off, and the youth, haggard and lean, lay before them. They nourished him as best they could, and, when well recovered, sent him home to join his people again and render them happy. Clad in his own fine garments, happy of countenance and handsome as before, and, according to his regular custom, bearing a Deer on his back, returned the youth to his people, and there he lived most happily.

As I have said, this was in the days of the ancients, and it is because this youth lived so long with the Deer and became acquainted with their every way and their every word, and taught all that he knew to his children and to others whom he took into his friendship, that we have today a class of menthe Sacred Hunters of our tribe, --who surpassingly understand the ways and the language of the Deer.

Thus shortens my story.

Go Forward With Courage

When you are in doubt, be still, and wait;
when doubt no longer exists for you, then go forward with courage.
So long as mists envelop you, be still;
be still until the sunlight pours through and dispels the mists
-- as it surely will.
Then act with courage.

Ponca Chief White Eagle (1800's to 1914)

Bonus Stories

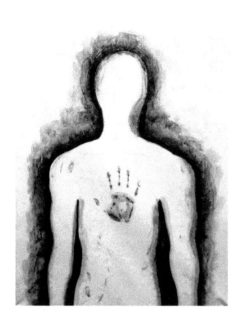

The Search for the Middle & the Hardening of the World

A Zuni Legend
Katharine Berry
Judson, Myths and
Legends of
California and the
Old Southwest, 1912

As it was with the first men and creatures, so it was with the world. It was young and unripe. Earthquakes shook the world and rent it. Demons and monsters of the underworld fled forth

Creatures became fierce, beasts of prey, and others turned timid, becoming their quarry. Wretchedness and hunger abounded and black magic. Fear was everywhere among them, so the people, in dread of their precious possessions, became wanderers, living on the seeds of grass, eaters of dead and slain things. Yet, guided by the Beloved Twain, they sought in the light and under the pathway of the Sun, the Middle of the world, over which alone they could find the earth at rest.

When the tremblings grew still for a time, the people paused at the First of Sitting Places. Yet they were still poor and defenseless and unskilled, and the world still moist and unstable. Demons and monsters fled from the earth in times of shaking, and threatened wanderers.

Then the Two took counsel of each other. The Elder said the earth must be made more stable for men and the valleys where their children rested. If they sent down their fire bolts of thunder, aimed to all the four regions, the earth would heave up and down, fire would, belch over the world and burn it, floods of hot water would sweep over it, smoke would blacken the daylight, but the earth would at last be safer for men.

So the Beloved Twain let fly the thunderbolts.

The mountains shook and trembled, the plains cracked and crackled under the floods and fires, and the hollow places, the only refuge of men and creatures, grew black and awful. At last thick rain fell, putting out the fires. Then water flooded the world, cutting deep trails through the mountains, and burying or uncovering the bodies of things and beings. Where they huddled together and were blasted thus, their blood gushed forth and flowed deeply, here in rivers, there in floods, for gigantic were they.

But the blood was charred and blistered and blackened by the fires into the black rocks of the lower mesas. There were vast plains of dust, ashes, and cinders, reddened like the mud of the hearth place. Yet many places behind and between the mountain terraces were unharmed by the fires, and even then green grew the trees and grasses and even flowers bloomed. Then the earth became more stable, and drier, and its lone places less fearsome since monsters of prey were changed to rock.

But ever and again the earth trembled and the people were troubled. "Let us again seek the Middle," they said. So they traveled far eastward to their second stopping place, the Place of Bare Mountains.

Again the world rumbled, and they traveled into a country to a place called Where-treeboles-stand-in-the-midst-of-waters. There they remained long, saying, "This is the Middle." They built homes there. At times they met people who had gone before, and thus they learned war. And many strange things happened there, as told in speeches of the ancient talk.

Then when the earth groaned again, the Twain bade them go forth, and they murmured. Many refused and perished miserably in their own homes, as do rats in falling trees, or flies in forbidden food.

But the greater number went forward until they came to Steam-mist-in-the-midst-ofwaters. And they saw the smoke of men's hearth fires and many houses scattered over the hills before them. When they came nearer, they challenged the people rudely, demanding who they were and why there, for in their last standing-place they had had touch of war.

"We are the People of the Seed," said the men of the hearth-fires, "born elder brothers of ye, and led of the gods."

"No," said our fathers, "we are led of the gods and we are the Seed People . . . "

Long lived the people in the town on the sunrise slope of the mountains of Kahluelawan, until the earth began to groan warningly again. Loath were they to leave the place of the Kaka and the lake of their dead. But the rumbling grew louder and the Twain Beloved called, and all together they journeyed eastward, seeking once more the Place of the Middle. But they grumbled amongst themselves, so when they came to a place of great promise, they said, "Let us stay here. Perhaps it may be the Place of the Middle."

So they built houses there, larger and stronger than ever before, and more perfect, for they were strong in numbers and wiser, though yet unperfected as men. They called the place "The Place of Sacred Stealing."

Long they dwelt there, happily, but growing wiser and stronger, so that, with their tails and dressed in the skins of animals, they saw they were rude and ugly.

In chase or in war, they were at a disadvantage, for they met older nations of men with whom they fought. No longer they feared the gods and monsters, but only their own kind. So therefore the gods called a council.

Changed shall ye be, oh our children, "cried the Twain." Ye shall walk straight in the pathways, clothed in garments, and without tails, that ye may sit more straight in council, and without webs to your feet, or talons on your hands."

So the people were arranged in procession like dancers. And the Twain with their weapons and fires of lightning shored off the forelocks hanging down over their faces, severed the talons, and slitted the webbed fingers and toes. Sore was the wounding and loud cried the foolish, when lastly the people were arranged in procession for the razing of their tails.

But those who stood at the end of the line, shrinking farther and farther, fled in their terror, climbing trees and high places, with loud chatter. Wandering far, sleeping ever in tree tops, in the far-away Summerland, they are sometimes

seen of far-walkers, long of tail and long handed, like
wizened men-children.

But the people grew in strength, and became more perfect,
and more than ever went to war. They grew vain. They had
reached the Place of the Middle. They said, "Let us not
wearily wander forth again even though the earth tremble
and the Twain bid us forth."

And even as they spoke, the mountain trembled and shook,
though far-sounding.

But as the people changed, changed also were the Twain,
small and misshapen, hard-favored and unyielding of will,
strong of spirit, evil and bad. They taught the people to war,
and led them far to the eastward.

At last the people neared, in the midst of the plains to the
eastward, great towns built in the heights. Great were the
fields and possessions of this people, for they knew how to
command and carry the waters, bringing new soil. And this,
too, without hail or rain. So our ancients, hungry with long
wandering for new food, were the more greedy and often
gave battle.

It was here that the Ancient Woman of the Elder People,
who carried her heart in her rattle and was deathless of
wounds in the body, led the enemy, crying out shrilly. So it
fell out ill for our fathers. For, moreover, thunder raged and
confused their warriors, rain descended and blinded them,
stretching their bow strings of sinew and quenching the
flight of their arrows as the flight of bees is quenched by
the sprinkling plume of the honey-hunter. But they devised
bow strings of yucca and the Two Little Ones sought
counsel of the Sun-father who revealed the life-secret of the
Ancient Woman and the magic powers over the under-fires

of the dwellers of the mountains, so that our enemy in the mountain town was overmastered. And because our people found in that great town some hidden deep in the cellars, and pulled them out as rats are pulled from a hollow cedar, and found them blackened by the fumes of their war magic, yet wiser than the common people, they spared them and received them into their next of kin of the Black Corn.

But the tremblings and warnings still sounded, and the people searched for the stable Middle.

Now they called a great council of men and the beasts, birds, and insects of all kinds. After a long council it was said, "Where is Water-skate? He has six legs, all very long. Perhaps he can feel with them to the uttermost of the six regions, and point out the very Middle."

So Water-skate was summoned. But lo! It was the Sun-father in his likeness which appeared. And he lifted himself to the zenith and extended his finger feet to all the six regions, so that they touched the north, the great waters; the west, and the south, and the east, the great waters; and to the northeast the waters above. and to the southwest the waters below. But to the north his finger foot grew cold, so he drew it in.

Then gradually he settled down upon the earth and said, "Where my heart rests, mark a spot, and build a town of the Mid-most, for there shall be the Mid-most Place of the Earth-mother."

And his heart rested over the middle of the plain and valley of Zuni. And when he drew in his finger-legs, lo! there were the trail-roads leading out and in like stays of a spider's nest, into and from the mid-most place he had covered.

Here because of their good fortune in finding the stable Middle, the priest father called the town the Abiding-place-of-happy-fortune.

The Beginning of Newness

A Zuni Legend
Katharine Berry
Judson, Myths and
Legends of California
and the Old
Southwest, 1912

Before the beginning of the New-making, the All-father Father alone had being. Through ages there was nothing else except black darkness.

In the beginning of the New-making, the All-father Father thought outward in space, and mists were created and up-lifted. Thus through his knowledge he made himself the Sun who was thus created and is the great Father. The dark spaces brightened with light. The cloud mists thickened and became water.

From his flesh, the Sun-father created the Seed-stuff of worlds, and he himself rested upon the waters. And these two, the Four-fold-containing Earth-mother and the All-covering Sky-father, the surpassing beings, with power of changing their forms even as smoke changes in the wind, were the father and mother of the soul beings.

Then as man and woman spoke these two together.

"Behold!" said Earth-mother, as a great terraced bowl appeared at hand, and within it water, "This shall be the home of my tiny children. On the rim of each world-country in which they wander, terraced mountains shall stand, making in one region many mountains by which one country shall be known from another."

Then she spat on the water and struck it and stirred it with her fingers. Foam gathered about the terraced rim, mounting higher and higher. Then with her warm breath she blew across the terraces. White flecks of foam broke away and floated over the water. But the cold breath of Sky-father shattered the foam and it fell downward in fine mist and spray.

Then Earth-mother spoke:

"Even so shall white clouds float up from the great waters at the borders of the world, and clustering about the mountain terraces of the horizon, shall be broken and hardened by thy cold. Then will they shed downward, in rain-spray, the water of life, even into the hollow places of my lap. For in my lap shall nestle our children, man-kind and creature-kind, for warmth in thy coldness."

So even now the trees on high mountains near the clouds and Sky-father, crouch low toward Earth mother for warmth and protection. Warm is Earth-mother, cold our Sky-father.

Then Sky-father said, "Even so. Yet I, too, will be helpful to our children." Then he spread his hand out with the palm downward and into all the wrinkles of his hand he set the semblance of shining yellow corn-grains; in the dark of the early world-dawn they gleamed like sparks of fire. "See," he said, pointing to the seven grains between his thumb and four fingers, "our children shall be guided by these when the Sun-father is not near and thy terraces are as darkness itself. Then shall our children be guided by lights." So Sky-father created the stars. Then he said, "And even as these grains gleam up from the water, so shall seed grain like them spring up from the earth when touched by water, to nourish our children." And thus they created the seed-corn. And in many other ways they devised for their children, the soul-beings.

But the first children, in a cave of the earth, were unfinished. The cave was of sooty blackness, black as a chimney at night time, and foul. Loud became their murmurings and lamentations, until many sought to escape, growing wiser and more man-like.

But the earth was not then as we now see it. Then Sun-father sent down two sons (sons also of the Foam-cap), the Beloved Twain, Twin Brothers of Light, yet Elder and Younger, the Right and the Left, like to question and answer in deciding and doing. To them the Sun-father imparted his own wisdom.

He gave them the great cloud-bow, and for arrows the thunderbolts of the four quarters. For buckler, they had the fog-making shield, spun and woven of the floating clouds and spray. The shield supports its bearer, as clouds are supported by the wind, yet hides its bearer also. And he gave to them the fathership and control of men and of all creatures.

Then the Beloved Twain, with their great cloud-bow lifted the Sky-father into the vault of the skies, that the earth might become warm and fitter for men and creatures. Then along the sun-seeking trail, they sped to the mountains westward. With magic knives they spread open the depths of the mountain and uncovered the cave in which dwelt the unfinished men and creatures. So they dwelt with men, learning to know them, and seeking to lead them out.

Now there were growing things in the depths, like grasses and vines. So the Beloved Twain breathed on the stems, growing tall toward the light as grass is wont to do, making them stronger, and twisting them upward until they formed a great ladder by which men and creatures ascended to a second cave.

Up the ladder into the second cave-world, men and the beings crowded, following closely the Two Little but Mighty Ones. Yet many fell back and were lost in the darkness. They peopled the under-world from which they escaped in after time, amid terrible earth shakings.

In this second cave it was as dark as the night of a stormy season, but larger of space and higher. Here again men and the beings increased, and their complainings grew loud. So the Twain again increased the growth of the ladder, and again led men upward, not all at once, but in six bands, to become the fathers of the six kinds of men, the yellow, the tawny gray, the red, the white, the black, and the mingled. And this time also many were lost or left behind.

Now the third great cave was larger and lighter, like a valley in starlight. And again they increased in number. And again the Two led them out into a fourth cave.

Here it was light like dawning, and men began to perceive and to learn variously, according to their natures, wherefore the Twain taught them first to seek the Sun-father.

Then as the last cave became filled and men learned to understand, the Two led them forth again into the great upper world, which is the World of Knowing Seeing.

The Origin of the Society of Rattlesnakes

A Zuni Legend
Frank Hamilton
Cushing, Zuni Folk
Tales, 1901

In very ancient times, there lived at Tâ'ia,' below the Zuñi Mountains, an old shíwani or priest-chief, who had a young son named Héasailuhtiwa ("Metal-hand"), famed throughout the land of the Zuñis for his success in hunting.

When very young, this lad had said to his parents: "My old ones, let me go away from the home of my fathers and dwell by myself."

"Why do you, a young boy, wish to go and dwell by yourself, my son? Know you not that you would fare but badly, for you are careless and forgetful? No, no! remain with us, that we may care for you."

But the boy answered: "Why should I fare badly? Can I not hunt my own game and roast the meat over the fire? It is because you never care to have me go forth alone that I wish to live by myself, for I long to travel far and hunt deer in the mountains of many countries: yet whenever I start forth you call me back, and it is painful to my longing thoughts thus to be held back when I would go forward."

It was not until the lad had spoken thus again and again, and once more, that the parents sadly yielded to his wish. They insisted, however, much to the boy's displeasure, that his younger sister, Waíasialuhtitsa, should go with him, only to look after his house, and to remind him here and there, at times, of his forgetfulness.

So the brother and sister chose the lofty rooms of a high house in the upper part of the pueblo and lived there.

The boy each day went out hunting and failed not each time to bring in slain animals, while the sister cooked for him and looked after the house. Yet, although the boy was a great hunter, he never sacrificed to the Deer he had slain, nor to the Gods of Prey who delight in aiding the hunter who renews them; for the lad was forgetful and careless of all things.

One day he went forth over the mountain toward the north, until he came to the Waters of the Bear. There he started up a huge Buck, and, finding the trail, followed it far toward the northward. Yet, although swift of foot, the youth could not overtake the running Deer, and thus it happened that he went on and on, past mesas, valleys, and mountains, until he came to the brink of a great river which flows westward from the north.

On the banks of this great river grew forests of cottonwood, and into the thickets of these forests led the trail, straight toward the river bank. just as the young man was about to follow the track to the bank, he thought he saw under a large tree in the midst of the thickets the form of the Deer, so, bending very low, he ran around close to the bank, and came up between the river and the thicket.

As he guardedly approached the tree, his eyes now following the track, now glancing up, he discovered a richly dressed, handsome young man, who called out to him: "How art thou these days, and whither art thou going?"

The young man straightened up, and quickly drawing his breath, replied: "I am hunting a Deer whose tracks I have followed all the way from the Waters of the Bear."

"Indeed!" exclaimed the stranger, "and where has thy Deer gone?"

"I know not," replied the youth, "for here are his tracks." Then he observed that they led to the place where the stranger was sitting, and the latter at the same time remarked:

"I am the Deer, and it was as I would have it that I enticed thee hither."

"Hai-í!" exclaimed the young man.

"Aye," continued the stranger. "Alas! alas! thou forgetful one! Thou hast day after day chased my children over the plains and slain them; thou hast made thyself happy of their flesh, and of their flesh added unto thine own meat and that of thy kindred; but, alas! thou hast been forgetful and careless, and not once hast thou given unto their souls the comfort of that which they yearn for and need. Yet hast thou had good fortune in the chase. At last the Sun-father has listened to the supplications of my children and commanded that I bring thee here, and here have I brought thee. Listen! The Sun-father commands that thou shalt visit him in his house at the western end of the world, and these are his instructions."

"Indeed! Well, I suppose it must be, and it is well!" exclaimed the young man.

"And," continued the Deer-being, "thou must hasten home

and call thy father. Tell him to summon his Pithlan Shíwani (Priest of the Bow, or Warrior) and command him that he shall instruct his children to repair to the rooms of sacred things and prepare plumed prayer-sticks for the Sun-father, the Moon-mother, and the Great Ocean, and red plumes of sacrifice for the Beings of Prey; that fully they must prepare everything, for thou, their child and father, shalt visit the home of the Sun-father, and in payment for thy forgetfulness and carelessness shalt render him, and the Moon-mother, and the Beings of the Great Ocean, plumes of sacrifice. "

"Hasten home, and tell thy father these things. Then tell thy sister to prepare sweetened meal of parched corn to serve as the food of thy journey, and pollen of the flowers of corn; and ask thy mother to prepare great quantities of new cotton, and, making all these things into bundles, thou must summon some of thy relatives, and come to this tree on the fourth day from this day."

"Make haste, for thou art swift of foot, and tell all these things to thy father; he, will understand thee, for is he not a priest-chief? Hast thou knives of flint?"

"Yes," said the young man, "my father has many."

"Select from them two," said the Deer-being--"a large one and a smaller one; and when thou hast returned to this place, cut down with the larger knife yonder great tree, and with the smaller knife hollow it out. Leave the large end entire, and for the smaller end thou must make a round door, and around the inside of the smaller end cut a notch that shall be like a terrace toward the outside, but shall slope from within that thou mayest close it from the inside with the round door; then pad the inside with cotton, and make in the bottom a padding thicker than the rest; but leave space that thou mayest lie thy length, or sit up and eat."

"And in the top cut a hole larger inside than out, that thou mayest close it from the inside with a plug of wood. Then when thou hast placed the sweetened meal of parched corn inside, and the plumed prayer-sticks and the sacred pollen of corn-flowers, then enter thyself and close the door in the end and the hole in the top that thy people may roll thee into the river. Thou wilt meet strange beings on thy way. Choose from amongst them whom thou shalt have as a companion, and proceed, as thy companion shall direct, to the great mountain where the Sun enters. Haste and tell thy father these things." And ere the youth could say, "Be it well," and, "I will," the Deer-being had vanished, and he lifted up his face and started swiftly for the home of his fathers.

At sunset the sister looked forth from her high house-top, but nowhere could she see her brother coming. She turned at last to enter, thinking and saying to her breast: "Alas! what did we not think and guess of his carelessness." But just as the country was growing dim in the darkness, the young man ran breathlessly in, and, greeting his sister, sat down in the doorway.

The sister wondered that he had no deer or other game, but placed a meal before him, and, when he had done, herself ate. But the young man remained silent until she had finished, then he said: "Younger sister, I am weary and would sit here; do you go and call father, for I would speak to him of many things."

So the sister cleared away the food and ran to summon the father. Soon she returned with the old man, who, sighing, "Ha hua!" from the effort of climbing, greeted his son and sat down, looking all about the room for the fresh deer-meat; but, seeing none, he asked: "What and wherefore hast thou summoned me, my son?"

"It is this," replied the son, and he related all that had been told him by the Deer-being, describing the magnificent dress, the turquoise and shell ear-rings, necklaces, and wristlets of the handsome stranger.

"Certainly," replied the father. "It is well; for as the Sun-father hath directed the Deer-being, thus must it be done." Then he forthwith went away and commanded his Priest of the Bow, who, mounting to the topmost house, directed the elders and priests of the tribe, saying: Ye, our children, listen! Ye I will this day inform, our child, our father, He of the strong hand, He who so hunts the Deer, goes unto the Sunset world, Goes, our Sun-father to greet Gather at the sacred houses, bring thy prayer-sticks, twines, and feathers, and prepare for him, For the Sun-father, For the Moon-mother, For the Great Ocean, For the Prey-beings, plumes and treasures. Hasten, hasten, ye our children, in the morning!"

So the people gathered in the kiwetsiwe and sacred houses next morning and began to make prayer-plumes, while the sister of the young man and her relatives made sweet parched cornmeal and gathered pollen. Toward evening all was completed. The young man summoned his relatives, and chose his four uncles to accompany him. Then he spread enough cotton-wool out to cover the floor, and, gathering it up, made it into a small bundle. The sweet meal filled a large sack of buckskin, and he took also a little sack of sacred red paint and the black warrior paint with little shining particles in it. Then he bade farewell to his lamenting people and rested for the evening journey.

Next morning, escorted by priests, the young man, arrayed in garments of embroidered white cotton and carrying his plumes in his arms, started out of the town, and, accompanied only by his four uncles, set out over the mountains. On the third day they reached the forest on the bank of the great river and encamped.

Then the young man left the camp of his uncles and went alone into the forest, and, choosing the greatest tree he could find, hacked midway through it with his great flint knife. The next day he cut the other half and felled it, when he found it partly hollow. So with his little knife he began to cut it as he had been directed, and made the round door for it and the hole through the top. With his bundle of cotton, he padded it everywhere inside until it was thickly coated and soft, and he made a bed on the bottom as thick as himself.

When all was ready and he had placed his food and plumes inside, he called his uncles and showed them the hollow log. "In this," said he, "I am to journey to the western home of our Sun-father. When I have entered and closed the round door tightly and put the plug into the upper hole securely, do ye, never thinking of me, roll the log over and over to the high brink of the river, and, never regarding consequences, push it into the water." Then it was that the uncles all lamented and tried to dissuade him; but he persisted, and they bade him "Go," as forever, "for," said they, "could one think of journeying even to the end of the earth and across the waters that embrace the world without perishing?"

Then, hastily embracing each of them, the young man entered his log, and, securely fastening the door from the inside, and the plug, called out (they heard but faintly), "Kesi!" which means "All is ready."

Sorrowfully and gently they rolled the log over and over to the high river bank, and, hesitating a moment, pushed it off with anxious eyes and closed mouths into the river. Eagerly they watched it as it tumbled end-over-end and down into the water with a great splash, and disappeared under the waves, which rolled one after another across to the opposite banks of the river. But for a long time they saw nothing of it. After a while, far off, speeding on toward the Western Waters of the World, they saw the log rocking along on the rushing waters until it passed out of sight, and they sadly turned toward their homes under the Mountains of the South.

When the log had ceased rocking and plunging, the young man cautiously drew out the plug, and, finding that no water flowed in, peered out. A ray of sunlight slanted in, and by that he knew it was not yet midday, and he could see a round piece of sky and clouds through the hole. By-and-by the ray of sunlight came straight down, and then after a while slanted the other way, and finally toward evening it ceased to shine in, and then the youth took out some of his meal and ate his supper.

When after a while he could see the stars, and later the Hanging Lines [the sword-belt of Orion], he knew it was time to rest, so he lay down to sleep.

Thus, day after day, he travelled until he knew he was out on the Great Waters of the World, for no longer did his log strike against anything or whirl around, nor could he see, through the chink, leaves of overhanging trees, nor rocks and banks of earth. On the tenth morning, when he looked up through the hole, he saw that the clouds did not move, and wondering at this, kicked at his log, but it would not move. Then he peered out as far as he could and saw rocks and trees. When he tried to rock his log, it remained firm, so he determined to open the door at the end.

Now, in reality, his log had been cast high up on the shore of a great mountain that rose out of the waters; and this mountain was the home of the Rattlesnakes. A Rattlesnake maiden was roaming along the shore just as the young man was about to open the door of his log. She espied the curious vessel, and said to herself in thought: "What may this be? Ah, yes, and who? Ah, yes, the mortal who was to come; it must be he!" Whereupon she hastened to the shore and tapped on the log.

"Art thou come?" she asked.

"Aye," replied the youth. "Who may you be, and where am I?"

"You are landed on the Island of the Rattlesnakes, and I am one of them. The other side of the mountain here is where our village is. Come out and go with me, for my old ones have expected you long."

"Is it dry, surely?" asked the young man.

"Why, yes! Here you are high above the waters."

Thereupon the young man opened from the inside his door, and peered out. Surely enough, there he was high among the rocks and sands. Then he looked at the Rattlesnake maiden, and scarcely believed she was what she called herself, for she was a most beautiful young woman, and like a daughter of men. Yet around her waist--she was dressed in cotton mantles--was girt a rattlesnake-skin which was open at the breast and on the crown of the head.

"Come with me," said the maiden; and she led the way over the mountain and across to a deep valley, where terrible

Serpents writhed and gleamed in the sunlight so thickly that they seemed, with their hissing and rattling, like a dry mat shaken by the wind. The youth drew back in horror, but the maiden said: "Fear not; they will neither harm you nor frighten you more, for they are my people."

Whereupon she commanded them to fall back and make a pathway for the young man and herself; and they tamely obeyed her commands. Through the opening thus made they passed down to a cavern, on entering which they found a great room. There were great numbers of Rattlesnake people, old and young, gathered in council, for they knew of the coming of the young man. Around the walls of their houses were many pegs and racks with serpent skins hanging on them--skins like the one the young girl wore as a girdle. The elders arose and greeted the youth, saying: "Our child and our father, comest thou, comest thou happily these many days?"

"Aye, happily," replied the youth.

And after a feast of strange food had been placed before the young man, and he had eaten a little, the elders said to him: "Knowest thou whither thou goest, that the way is long and fearful, and to mortals unknown, and that it will be but to meet with poverty that thou journeyest alone? Therefore, have we assembled to await thy coming and in order that thou shouldst journey preciously, we have decided to ask thee to choose from amongst us whom thou shalt have for a companion."

"It is well, my fathers," said the young man, and, casting his eyes about the council to find which face should be kindest to him, he chose the maiden, and said: "Let it be this one, for she found me and loved me in that she gently and without fear brought me into your presence."

And the girl said: "It is well, and I will go."

Instantly the grave and dignified elders, the happy-faced youths and maidens, the kind-eyed matrons, all reached up for their serpent skins, and, passing them over their persons, --lo! in the time of the telling of it, the whole place was filled with writhing and hissing Serpents and the din of their rattles. In horror the young man stood against the wall like a hollow stalk, and the Serpent maiden, going to each of the members of the council, extracted from each a single fang, which she wrapped together in a piece of fabric, until she had a great bundle.

Then she passed her hand over her person, and lo! she became a beautiful human maiden again, holding in her hand a rattlesnake skin. Then taking up the bundle of fangs, she said to the young man: "Come, for I know the way and will guide you,"--and the young man followed her to the shore where his log lay.

"Now," said she, "wait while I fix this log anew, that it may be well," and she bored many little holes all over the log, and into these holes she inserted the crooked fangs, so that they all stood slanting toward the rear, like the spines on the back of a porcupine.

When she had done this, she said: "First I will enter, for there may not be room for two, and in order that I may make myself like the space I enter, I will lay on my dress again. Do you, when I have entered, enter also, and with your feet kick the log down to the shore waters, when you must quickly close the door and the waters will take us abroad upon themselves."

In an instant she had passed into her serpent form again and crawled into the log. The young man did as he was bidden, and as he closed the door a wave bore them gently out upon the waters. Then, as the young man turned to look upon his companion coiled so near him, he drew back in horror.

"Why do you fear?" asked the Rattlesnake.

"I know not, but I fear you; perhaps, though you speak gently, you will, when I sleep, bite me and devour my flesh, and it is with thoughts of this that I have fear."

"Ah, no!" replied the maiden, "but, that you may not fear, I will change myself." And so saying, she took off her skin, and, opening the upper part of the door, hung the skin on the fangs outside.

Finally, toward noon-time, the youth prepared his meal food, and placing some before the maiden, asked her to eat.

"Ah, no! alas, I know not the food of mortals. Have you not with you the yellow dust of the corn-flower?"

"Aye, that I have," said the young man, and producing a bag, opened it and asked the girl: "How shall I feed it to you?"

"Scatter it upon the cotton, and by my knowledge I will gather it."

Then the young man scattered a great quantity on the cotton, wondering how the girl would gather it up. But the maiden opened the door, and taking down the skin changed herself to a serpent, and passing to and fro over the pollen, received it all within her scales. Then she resumed her human form again and hung the skin up as before.

Thus they floated until they came to the great forks of the Mighty Waters of the World, and their floating log was guided into the southern branch. And on they floated toward the westward for four months from the time when the uncles had thrown him into the river.

One day the maiden said to the youth: "We are nearing our journey's end, and, as I know the way, I will guide you. Hold yourself hard and ready, for the waters will cast our house high upon the shores of the mountain wherein the Sun enters, and these shores are inaccessible because so smooth."

Then the log was cast high above the slippery bank, and when the waters receded there it remained, for the fangs grappled it fast.

Then said the maiden: "Let us now go out. Fear not for your craft, for the fangs will hold it fast; it matters little how high the waves may roll, or how steep and slippery the bank."

Then, taking in his arms the sacred plumes which his people had prepared for him, he followed the girl far up to the doorway in the Mountain of the Sea. Out of it grew a great ladder of giant rushes, by the side of which stood an enormous basket-tray. Very fast approached the Sun, and soon the Sun-father descended the ladder, and the two voyagers followed down. They were gently greeted by a kind old woman, the grandmother of the Sun, and were given seats at one side of a great and wonderfully beautiful room.

Then the Sun-father approached some pegs in the wall and from them suspended his bow and quiver, and his bright sun-shield, and his wonderful travelling dress Behold! there stood, kindly smiling before the youth and maiden, the most magnificent and gentle of beings in the world-the

Sun-father.

Then the Sun-father greeted them, and, turning to a great package which he had brought in, opened it and disclosed thousands of shell beads, red and white, and thousands more of brilliant turquoises.

These he poured into the great tray at the door-side, and gave them to the grandmother, who forthwith began to sort them with great rapidity. But, ere she had done, the Sun-father took them from her; part of them he took out with unerring judgment and cast them abroad into the great waters as we cast sacred prayer-meal. The others he brought below and gave them to the grandmother for safe-keeping.

Then he turned once more to the youth and the maiden, and said to the former: "So thou hast come, my child, even as I commanded. It is well, and I am thankful." Then, in a stern and louder voice, which yet sounded like the voice of a father, he asked: "Hast thou brought with thee that whereby we are made happy with our children?"

And the young man said: "Aye, I have."

"It is well; and if it be well, then shalt thou precious be; for knowest thou not that I recognize the really good from the evil, --even of the thoughts of men, --and that I know the prayer and sacrifice that is meant, from the words and treasures of those who do but lie in addressing them to me, and speak and act as children in a joke? Behold the treasure which I brought with me from the cities of mankind today! Some of them I cherished preciously, for they are the gifts to me of good hearts and I treasure them that I may return them in good fortune and blessing to those who gave them."

"But some thou sawest I cast abroad into the great waters that they may again be gathered up and presented to me; for they were the gifts of double and foolish hearts, and as such cannot be treasured by me nor returned unto those who gave them. Bring forth, my child, the plumes and gifts thou hast brought. Thy mother dwelleth in the next room, and when she appeareth in this, thou shalt with thine own hand present to her thy sacrifice."

So the youth, bowing his head, unwrapped his bundle and laid before the Sun-father the plumes he had brought. And the Sun-father took them and breathed upon them and upon the youth, and said: "Thanks, this day. Thou hast straightened thy crooked thoughts."

And when the beautiful Mother of Men, the Moon-mother-- the wife of the Sun-father-appeared, the boy placed before her the plumes he had brought, and she, too, breathed upon them, and said: "Thanks, this day," even as the Sun-father had.

Then the Sun-father turned to the youth and said: "Thou shalt join me in my journey round the world, that thou mayest see the towns and nations of mankind--my children; that thou mayest realize how many are my children. Four days shalt thou join me in my journeyings, and then shalt thou return to the home of thy fathers."

And the young man said: "It is well!" but he turned his eyes to the maiden.

"Fear not, my child," added the Father, "she shall sit preciously in my house until we have returned."

And after they had feasted, the Sun-father again enrobed himself, and the youth he dressed in appearance as he himself was dressed. Then, taking the sun-dress from the wall, he led the way down through the four great apartments of the world, and came out into the Lower Country of the Earth.

Behold! as they entered that great world, it was filled with snow and cold below, and the tracks of men led out over great white plains, and as they passed the cities of these nether countries people strange to see were clearing away the snow from their housetops and doorways.

And so they journeyed to the other House of the Sun, and, passing up through the four great rooms, entered the home of the aunts of the Sun-father; and here, too, the young man presented plumes of prayer and sacrifice to the inmates, and received their thanks and blessings.

Again they started together on their journey; and behold! as they came out into the World of Daylight, the skies below them were filled with the rain of summer-time.

Across the great world they journeyed, and they saw city after city of men, and many tribes of strange peoples. Here they were engaged in wars and in wasting the lives of one another; there they were dying of famine and disease; and more of misery and poverty than of happiness saw the young man among the nations of men. "For," said the Sun-father, "these be, alas! my children, who waste their lives in foolishness, or slay one another in useless anger; yet they are brothers to one another, and I am the father of all."

Thus journeyed they four days; and each evening when they returned to the home where the Sun-father enters, he gave to his grandmother the great package of treasure which his children among men had sacrificed to him, and each day he cast the treasures of the bad and double-hearted into the great waters.

On the fourth day, when they had entered the western home of the Sun-father, said the latter to the youth: "Thy task is meted out and finished; thou shalt now return unto the home of thy fathers--my children below the mountains of Shíwina. How many days, thinkest thou, shalt thou journey?"

"Many days more than ten," replied the youth with a sigh.

"Ah! no, my child," said the Sun-father. "Listen; thou shalt in one day reach the banks of the river whence thou camest. Listen! Thou shalt take this, my shaft of strong lightning; thou shalt grasp its neck with firm hands, and as thou extendest it, it will stretch out far to thy front and draw thee more swiftly than the arrow's flight through the water. Take with thee this quiver of unerring arrows, and this strong bow, that by their will thou mayest seek life; but forget not thy sacrifices nor that they are to be made with true word and a faithful heart. Take also with thee thy guide and companion, the Rattlesnake maiden. When thou hast arrived at the shore of the country of her people, let go the lightning, and it will land thee high."

"On the morrow I will journey slowly, that ere I be done rising thou mayest reach the home of the maiden. There thou must stop but briefly, for thy fathers, the Rattle-tailed Serpents, will instruct thee, and to their counsel thou must pay strict heed, for thus only will it be well. Thou shalt present to them the plumes of the Prey-beings thou bringest, and when thou hast presented these, thou must continue thy journey. Rest thou until the morrow, and early as the light speed hence toward the home of thy fathers. May all days find ye, children, happy." With this, the Sun-father, scarce listening to the prayers and thanks of the youth and maiden, vanished below.

Thus, when morning approached, the youth and the maiden entered the hollow house and closed it. Scarce did the youth grasp the lightning when, drawn by the bright shaft, the log shot far out into the great waters and was skimming, too fast to be seen, toward the home of the Rattle-tailed Serpents.

And the Sun had but just climbed above the mountains of this world of daylight when the little tube was thrown high above the banks of the great island whither they were journeying.

Then the youth and the maiden again entered the council of the Rattlesnakes, and when they saw the shining black paint on his face they asked that they too might paint their faces like his own; but they painted their cheeks awkwardly, as to this day may be seen; for all rattlesnakes are painted unevenly in the face. Then the young man presented to each the plumes he had brought, and told the elders that he would return with their maiden to the home of his father.

"Be it well, that it may be well," they replied; and they thanked him with delight for the treasure-plumes he had bestowed upon them.

"Go ye happily all days," said the elders. "Listen, child, and father, to our words of advice. But a little while, and thou wilt reach the bank whence thou started. Let go the shaft of lightning, and, behold, the tube thou hast journeyed with will plunge far down into the river. Then shalt thou journey with this our maiden three days. Care not to embrace her, for if thou doest this, it will not be well. journey ye preciously, our children, and may ye be happy one with the other."

So again they entered their hollow log and, before entering, the maiden placed her rattlesnake skin as before on the fangs. With incredible swiftness the lightning drew them up the great surging river to the banks where the cottonwood forests grow, and when the lad pressed the shaft it landed them high among the forest trees above the steep bank. Then the youth pressed the lightning-shaft with all his might, and the log was dashed into the great river.

While yet he gazed at the bounding log, behold! the fangs which the maiden had fixed into it turned to living serpents; hence today, throughout the whole great world, from the Land of Summer to the Waters of Sunset, are found the Rattlesnakes and their children.

Then the young man journeyed with the maiden southward; and on the way, with the bow and arrows the Sun-father had given him, he killed game, that they might have meat to eat. Nor did he forget the commandments of his Sun-father. At night he built a fire in a forest of piñons, and made a bower for the maiden near to it; but she could not sit there, for she feared the fire, and its light pained her eyes. Nor could she eat at first of the food he cooked for her, but only tasted a few mouthfuls of it. Then the young man made a bed for her under the trees, and told her to rest peacefully, for he would guard her through the night.

And thus they journeyed and rested until the fourth day, when at evening they entered the town under the mountains of Shíwina and were happily welcomed by the father, sister, and relatives of the young man. Blessed by the old priest-chief, the youth and the maiden dwelt with the younger sister Waíasialuhtitsa, in the high house of the upper part of the town. And the boy was as before a mighty hunter, and the maiden at last grew used to the food and ways of mortals.

After they had thus lived together for a long time, there were born of the maiden two children, twins.

Wonderful to relate, these children grew to the power of wandering, in a single day and night; and hence, when they appeared suddenly on the housetops and in the plazas, people said to one another:

"Who are these strange people, and whence came they?"-- and talked much after the manner of our foolish people. And the other little children in the town beat them and quarreled with them, as strange children are apt to do with strange children. And when the twins ran in to their mother, crying and complaining, the poor young woman was saddened; so she said to the father when he returned from hunting in the evening:

"Ah!, 'their father,' it is not well that we remain longer here. No, alas! I must return to the country of my fathers, and take with me these little ones," and, although the father prayed her not, she said only: "It must be," and he was forced to consent.

Then for four days the Rattlesnake woman instructed him in the prayers and chants of her people, and she took him forth and showed him the medicines whereby the bite of her fathers might be assuaged, and how to prepare them. Again and again the young man urged her not to leave him, saying: "The way is long and filled with dangers. How, alas! will you reach it in safety?"

"Fear not," said she: "go with me only to the shore of the great river, and my fathers will come to meet me and take me home."

Sadly, on the last morning, the father accompanied his wife

and children to the forests of the great river. There she said he must not follow but as he embraced them he cried out:

"Ah, alas! my beautiful wife, my beloved children, flesh of my flesh, how shall I not follow ye?"

Then his wife answered: "Fear not, nor trouble thyself with sad thoughts. Whither we go thou canst not follow, for thou eatest cooked food (thou art a mortal); but soon thy fathers and mine will come for thee, and thou wilt follow us, never to return." Then she turned from him with the little children and was seen no more, and the young man silently returned to his home below the mountains of Shíwina.

It happened here and there in time that young men of his tribe were bitten by rattlesnakes; but the young man had only to suck their wounds, and apply his medicines, and sing his incantations and prayers, to cure them. Whenever this happened, he breathed the sacred breath upon them, and enjoined them to secrecy of the rituals and chants he taught them, save only to such as they should choose and teach the practice of their prayers.

Thus he had cured and taught eight, when one day he ascended the mountains for wood. There, alone in the forest, he was met and bitten by his fathers. Although he slowly and painfully crawled home, long ere he reached his town he was so swollen that the eight whom he had instructed tried in vain to cure him, and, bidding them cherish as a precious gift the knowledge of his beloved wife, he died.

Immediately his fathers met his breath and being and took them to the home of the Maiden of the Rattlesnakes and of his lost children. Need we ask why he was not cured by his disciples?

Thus it was in the days of the ancients, and hence today we have fathers amongst us to whom the dread bite of the rattlesnake need cause no sad thoughts, --the Tchi Kialikwe (Society of the Rattlesnakes).

Thus much and thus shortened is my story.

Origin of the Raven and the Macaw

A Zuni Legend
Katharine Berry Judson,
Myths and Legends of
California and the Old
Southwest, 1912

The priest who was named Yanauluha carried ever in his hand a staff which now in the daylight was plumed and covered with feathers - yellow, blue-green, red, white, black, and varied. Attached to it were shells, which made a song-like tinkle. The people when they saw it stretched out their hands and asked many questions.

Then the priest balanced it in his hand, and struck with it a hard place, and blew upon it. Amid the plumes appeared four round things-mere eggs they were. Two were blue like the sky and two dun-red like the flesh of the Earth-mother.

Then the people asked many questions; "These," said the priests, "are the seed of living beings. Choose which ye will follow. From two eggs shall come beings of beautiful plumage, colored like the grass and fruits of summer. Where they fly and ye follow, shall always be summer. Without toil, fields of food shall flourish. And from the other two eggs shall come evil beings, piebald, with white, without colors. And where these two shall fly and ye shall follow, winter strives with summer. Only by labor shall the fields yield fruit, and your children and theirs shall strive for the fruits. Which do ye choose?"

"The blue! The blue!" cried the people, and those who were strongest carried off the blue eggs, leaving the red eggs to those who waited. They laid the blue eggs with much gentleness in soft sand on the sunny side of a hill, watching day by day. They were precious of color; surely they would be the precious birds of the Summer-land. Then the eggs cracked and the birds came out, with open eyes and pin feathers under their skins.

"We chose wisely," said the people. "Yellow and blue, red and green, are their dresses, even seen through their skins." So they fed them freely of all the foods which men favor. Thus they taught them to eat all desirable food. But when the feathers appeared, they were black with white bandings. They were ravens. And they flew away croaking hoarse laughs and mocking our fathers.

But the other eggs became beautiful macaws, and were wafted by a toss of the priest's wand to the faraway Summer-land.

So those who had chosen the raven, became the Raven People. They were the Winter People and they were many and strong. But those who had chosen the macaw, became the Macaw People. They were the Summer People, and few in number, and less strong, but they were wiser because they were more deliberate. The priest Yanauluha, being wise, became their father, even as the Sun-father is among the little moons of the sky. He and his sisters were the ancestors of the priest-keepers of things.

The Search for the Corn Maidens

*A Zuni Legend
Katharine Berry
Judson, Myths and
Legends of California
and the Old
Southwest, 1912*

The people in their trouble called the two Master-Priests and said: "Who, now, think ye, should journey to seek our precious Maidens? Bethink ye! Who amongst the Beings is even as ye are, strong of will and good of eyes?"

Then they added, "There is our great elder brother and father, Eagle, he of the floating down and of the terraced tail-fan. Surely he is enduring of will and surpassing of sight."

"Yea. Most surely," said the fathers. "Go ye forth and beseech him."

Then the two sped north to Twin Mountain, where in a grotto high up among the crags, with his mate and his young, dwelt the Eagle of the White Bonnet.

They climbed the mountain, but behold! Only the eaglets were there. They screamed lustily and tried to hide themselves in the dark recesses. "Pull not our feathers, ye of hurtful touch, but wait. When we are older we will drop them for you even from the clouds."

"Hush," said the warriors. "Wait in peace. We seek not ye but thy father."

Then from afar, with a frown, came old Eagle. "Why disturb ye my featherlings?" he cried.

"Behold! Father and elder brother, we come seeking only the light of thy favor. Listen!"

Then they told him of the lost Maidens of the Corn, and begged him to search for them.

"Be it well with thy wishes," said Eagle. "Go ye before contentedly."

So the warriors returned to the council. But Eagle winged his way high into the sky. High, high, he rose, until he circled among the clouds, small-seeming and swift, like seed-down in a whirlwind. Through all the heights, to the north, to the west, to the south, and to the east, he circled and sailed. Yet nowhere saw he trace of the Corn Maidens.

Then he flew lower, returning. Before the warriors were rested, people heard the roar of his wings. As he alighted, the fathers said, "Enter thou and sit, oh brother, and say to us what thou hast to say." And they offered him the cigarette of the space relations.

When they had puffed the smoke toward the four points of the compass, and Eagle had purified his breath with smoke, and had blown smoke over sacred things, he spoke.

"Far have I journeyed, scanning all the regions. Neither bluebird nor woodrat can hide from my seeing," he said, snapping his beak. "Neither of them, unless they hide under bushes. Yet I have failed to see anything of the Maidens ye seek for. Send for my younger brother, the Falcon. Strong of flight is he, yet not so strong as I, and nearer the ground he takes his way ere sunrise."

Then the Eagle spread his wings and flew away to Twin Mountain. The Warrior-Priests of the Bow sped again fleetly over the plain to the westward for his younger brother, Falcon.

Sitting on an ant hill, so the warriors found Falcon. He paused as they approached, crying, "If ye have snare strings, I will be off like the flight of an arrow well plumed of our feathers! "

"No," said the priests. "Thy elder brother hath bidden us seek thee."

Then they told Falcon what had happened, and how Eagle had failed to find the Corn Maidens, so white and beautiful.

"Failed!" said Falcon. "Of course he failed. He climbs aloft to the clouds and thinks he can see under every bush and into every shadow, as sees the Sunfather who sees not with eyes. Go ye before."

Before the Warrior-Priests had turned toward the town, the Falcon had spread his sharp wings and was skimming off over the tops of the trees and bushes as though verily seeking for field mice or birds' nests. And the Warriors returned to tell the fathers and to await his coming.

But after Falcon had searched over the world, to the north and west, to the east and south, he too returned and was received as had been Eagle. He settled on the edge of a tray before the altar, as on the ant hill he settles today. When he had smoked and had been smoked, as had been Eagle, he told the sorrowing fathers and mothers that he had looked behind every copse and cliff shadow, but of the Maidens he had found no trace.

"They are hidden more closely than ever sparrow hid," he said. Then he, too, flew away to his hills in the west.

"Our beautiful Maiden Mothers," cried the matrons. "Lost, lost as the dead are they!"

"Yes," said the others. "Where now shall we seek them? The far-seeing Eagle and the close-searching Falcon alike have failed to find them."

"Stay now your feet with patience," said the fathers. Some of them had heard Raven, who sought food in the refuse and dirt at the edge of town, at daybreak.

"Look now," they said. "There is Heavy-nose, whose beak never fails to find the substance of seed itself, however little or well-hidden it be. He surely must know of the Corn Maidens. Let us call him."

So the warriors went to the river side. When they found Raven, they raised their hands, all weaponless.

"We carry no pricking quills," they called. "Blackbanded father, we seek your aid. Look now! The Mother-maidens of Seed whose substance is the food alike of thy people and our people, have fled away. Neither our grandfather the Eagle, nor his younger brother the Falcon, can trace them. We beg you to aid us or counsel us."

"Ka! ka!" cried the Raven. "Too hungry am I to go abroad fasting on business for ye. Ye are stingy! Here have I been since perching time, trying to find a throatful, but ye pick thy bones and lick thy bowls too clean for that, be sure."

"Come in, then, poor grandfather. We will give thee food to cat. Yea, and a cigarette to smoke, with all the ceremony."

"Say ye so?" said the Raven. He ruffled his collar and opened his mouth so wide with a lusty kaw-la-ka- that he might well have swallowed his own head. "Go ye before," he said, and followed them into the court of the dancers.

He was not ill to look upon. Upon his shoulders were bands of white cotton, and his back was blue, gleaming like the hair of a maiden dancer in the sunlight. The Master-Priest greeted Raven, bidding him sit and smoke.

"Ha! There is corn in this, else why the stalk of it?" said the Raven, when he took the cane cigarette of the far spaces and noticed the joint of it. Then he did as he had seen the Master-Priest do, only more greedily.

He sucked in such a throatful of the smoke, fire and all, that it almost strangled him. He coughed and grew giddy, and the smoke all hot and stinging went through every part of him. It filled all his feathers, making even his brown eyes bluer and blacker, in rings. It is not to be wondered at, the blueness of flesh, blackness of dress, and skinniness, yes, and tearfulness of eye which we see in the Raven to-day. And they are all as greedy of corn food as ever, for behold! No sooner had the old Raven recovered than he espied one of the ears of corn half hidden under the mantle-covers of the trays.

He leaped from his place laughing. They always laugh when they find anything, these ravens. Then he caught up the ear of corn and made off with it over the heads of the people and the tops of the houses, crying.

"Ha! ha! In this wise and in no other will ye find thy Seed Maidens."

But after a while he came back, saying, "A sharp eye have I for the flesh of the Maidens. But who might see their breathing-beings, ye dolts, except by the help of the Father of Dawn-Mist himself, whose breath makes breath of others seem as itself." Then he flew away cawing.

Then the elders said to each other, "It is our fault, so how dare we prevail on our father Paiyatuma to aid us? He warned us of this in the old time."

Suddenly, for the sun was rising, they heard Paiyatuma in his daylight mood and transformation. Thoughtless and loud, uncouth in speech, he walked along the outskirts of the village. He joked fearlessly even of fearful things, for all his words and deeds were the reverse of his sacred being. He sat down on a heap of vile refuse, saying he would have a feast.

"My poor little children," he said. But he spoke to aged priests and white-haired matrons.

"Good-night to you all," he said, though it was in full dawning. So he perplexed them with his speeches.

"We beseech thy favor, oh father, and thy aid, in finding our beautiful Maidens." So the priests mourned.

"Oh, that is all, is it? But why find that which is not lost, or summon those who will not come?"

Then he reproached them for not preparing the sacred plumes, and picked up the very plumes he had said were not there.

Then the wise Pekwinna, the Speaker of the Sun, took two plumes and the banded wing-tips of the turkey, and approaching Paiyatuma stroked him with the tips of the feathers and then laid the feathers upon his lips.

Then Paiyatuma became aged and grand and straight, as is a tall tree shorn by lightning. He said to the father:

"Thou are wise of thought and good of heart. Therefore, I will summon from Summer-land the beautiful Maidens that ye may look upon them once more and make offering of plumes in sacrifice for them, but they are lost as dwellers amongst ye."

Then he told them of the song lines and the sacred speeches and of the offering of the sacred plume wands, and then turned him about and sped away so fleetly that none saw him.

Beyond the first valley of the high plain to the southward Paiyatuma planted the four plume wands. First he planted the yellow, bending over it and watching it. When it ceased to flutter, the soft down on it leaned northward but moved not. Then he set the blue wand and watched it; then the white wand. The eagle down on them leaned to right and left and still northward, yet moved not.

Then farther on he planted the red wand, and bending low, without breathing, watched it closely. The soft down plumes began to wave as though blown by the breath of some small creature. Backward and forward, northward and southward they swayed, as if in time to the breath of one resting.

"'T is the breath of my Maidens in Summer-land, for the plumes of the southland sway soft to their gentle breathing.

So shall it ever be. When I set the down of my mists on the plains and scatter my bright beads in the northland, summer shall go thither from afar, borne on the breath of the Seed Maidens. Where they breathe, warmth, showers, and fertility shall follow with the birds of Summer-land, and the butterflies, northward over the world."

Then Paiyatuma arose and sped by the magic of his knowledge into the countries of Summer-land, -fled swiftly and silently as the soft breath he sought for, bearing his painted flute before him. And when he paused to rest, he played on his painted flute and the butterflies and birds sought him. So he sent them to seek the Maidens, following swiftly, and long before he found them he greeted them with the music of his songsound, even as the People of the Seed now greet them in the song of the dancers.

When the Maidens heard his music and saw his tall form in their great fields of corn, they plucked ears, each of her own kind, and with them filled their colored trays and over all spread embroidered mantles, - embroidered in all the bright colors and with the creature-songs of Summer-land. So they sallied forth to meet him and welcome him. Then he greeted them, each with the touch of his hands and the breath of his flute, and bade them follow him to the northland home of their deserted children.

So by the magic of their knowledge they sped back as the stars speed over the world at night time, toward the home of our ancients. Only at night and dawn they journeyed, as the dead do, and the stars also. So they came at evening in the full of the last moon to the Place of the Middle, bearing their trays of seed.

Glorious was Paiyatuma, as he walked into the courts of the dancers in the dusk of the evening and stood with folded

arms at the foot of the bow-fringed ladder of priestly
council, he and his follower Shutsukya. He was tall and
beautiful and banded with his own mists, and carried the
banded wings of the turkeys with which he had winged his
flight from afar, leading the Maidens, and followed as by
his own shadow by the black being of the corn-soot,
Shutsukya, who cries with the voice of the frost wind when
the corn has grown aged and the harvest is taken away.

And surpassingly beautiful were the Maidens clothed in the
white cotton and embroidered garments of Summer-land.

Then after long praying and chanting by the priests, the
fathers of the people, and those of the Seed and Water, and
the keepers of sacred things, the Maiden-mother of the
North advanced to the foot of the ladder. She lifted from
her head the beautiful tray of yellow corn and Paiyatama
took it. He pointed it to the regions, each in turn, and the
Priest of the North came and received the tray of sacred
seed.

Then the Maiden of the West advanced and gave up her
tray of blue corn. So each in turn the Maidens gave up their
trays of precious seed. The Maiden of the South, the red
seed; the Maiden of the East, the white seed; then the
Maiden with the black seed, and lastly, the tray of all-color
seed which the Priestess of Seed-and-All herself received.

And now, behold! The Maidens stood as before, she of the
North at the northern end, but with her face southward far
looking; she of the West, next, and lo! so all of them, with
the seventh and last, looking southward.

And standing thus, the darkness of the night fell around
them. As shadows in deep night, so these Maidens of the
Seed of Corn, the beloved and beautiful, were seen no more

of men.

And Paiyatuma stood alone, for Shutsukya walked now behind the Maidens, whistling shrilly, as the frost wind whistles when the corn is gathered away, among the lone canes and dry leaves of a gleaned field.

The Serpent of the Sea

A Zuni Legend
Frank Hamilton
Cushing, Zuni Folk
Tales, 1901

In the times of our forefathers, under Thunder Mountain was a village called K'iákime ("Home of the Eagles"). It is now in ruins; the roofs are gone, the ladders have decayed, the hearths grown cold.

But when it was all still perfect, and, as it were, new, there lived in this village a maiden, the daughter of the priest-chief. She was beautiful, but possessed of this peculiarity of character: There was a sacred spring of water at the foot of the terrace whereon stood the town.

We now call it the Pool of the Apaches; but then it was sacred to Kólowissi (the Serpent of the Sea). Now, at this spring the girl displayed her peculiarity, which was that of a passion for neatness and cleanliness of person and clothing.

She could not endure the slightest speck or particle of dust or dirt upon her clothes or person, and so she spent most of her time in washing all the things she used and in bathing herself in the waters of this spring.

Now, these waters, being sacred to the Serpent of the Sea, should not have been defiled in this way.

As might have been expected, Kólowissi became troubled and angry at the sacrilege committed in the sacred waters by the maiden, and he said: "Why does this maiden defile the sacred waters of my spring with the dirt of her apparel and the dun of her person? I must see to this."

So he devised a plan by which to prevent the sacrilege and to punish its author.

When the maiden came again to the spring, what should she behold but a beautiful little child seated amidst the waters, splashing them, cooing and smiling. It was the Sea Serpent, wearing the semblance of a child, --for a god may assume any form at its pleasure, you know. There sat the child, laughing and playing in the water.

The girl looked around in all directions--north, south, east, and west--but could see no one, nor any traces of persons who might have brought hither the beautiful little child.

She said to herself: "I wonder whose child this may be! It would seem to be that of some unkind and cruel mother, who has deserted it and left it here to perish. And the poor little child does not yet know that it is left all alone. Poor little thing! I will take it in my arms and care for it."

The maiden then talked softly to the young child, and took it in her arms, and hastened with it up the hill to her house, and, climbing up the ladder, carried the child in her arms into the room where she slept.

Her peculiarity of character, her dislike of all dirt or dust, led her to dwell apart from the rest of her family, in a room by herself above all of the other apartments.

She was so pleased with the child that when she had got

him into her room she sat down on the floor and played with him, laughing at his pranks and smiling into his face; and he answered her in baby fashion with cooings and smiles of his own, so that her heart became very happy and loving. So it happened that thus was she engaged for a long while and utterly unmindful of the lapse of time.

Meanwhile, the younger sisters had prepared the meal, and were awaiting the return of the elder sister.

"Where, I wonder, can she be?" one of them asked.

"She is probably down at the spring," said the old father; "she is bathing and washing her clothes, as usual, of course! Run down and call her."

But the younger sister, on going, could find no trace of her at the spring. So she climbed the ladder to the private room of this elder sister, and there found her, as has been told, playing with the little child. She hastened back to inform her father of what she had seen. But the old man sat silent and thoughtful. He knew that the waters of the spring were sacred.

When the rest of the family were excited, and ran to behold the pretty prodigy, he cried out, therefore: "Come back! come back! Why do you make fools of yourselves? Do you suppose any mother would leave her own child in the waters of this or any other spring? There is something more of meaning than seems in all this."

When they again went and called the maiden to come down to the meal spread for her, she could not be induced to leave the child.

"See! it is as you might expect," said the father. "A woman will not leave a child on any inducement; how much less her own."

The child at length grew sleepy. The maiden placed it on a bed, and, growing sleepy herself, at length lay by its side and fell asleep. Her sleep was genuine, but the sleep of the child was feigned. The child became elongated by degrees, as it were, fulfilling some horrible dream, and soon appeared as an enormous Serpent that coiled itself round and round the room until it was full of scaly, gleaming circles. Then, placing its head near the head of the maiden, the great Serpent surrounded her with its coils, taking finally its own tail in its mouth.

The night passed, and in the morning when the breakfast was prepared, and yet the maiden did not descend, and the younger sisters became impatient at the delay, the old man said: "Now that she has the child to play with, she will care little for aught else. That is enough to occupy the entire attention of any woman."

But the little sister ran up to the room and called. Receiving no answer, she tried to open the door; she could not move it, because the Serpent's coils filled the room and pressed against it. She pushed the door with all her might, but it could not be moved. She again and again called her sister's name, but no response came. Beginning now to be frightened, she ran to the skyhole over the room in which she had left the others and cried out for help.

They hastily joined her, --all save the old father, --and together were able to press the door sufficiently to get a glimpse of the great scales and folds of the Serpent. Then the women all ran screaming to the old father. The old man, priest and sage as he was, quieted them with these words: "I expected as much as this from the first report which you gave me.

It was impossible, as I then said, that a woman should be so foolish as to leave her child playing even near the waters of the spring. But it is not impossible, it seems, that one should be so foolish as to take into her arms a child found as this one was."

Thereupon he walked out of the house, deliberately and thoughtful, angry in his mind against his eldest daughter. Ascending to her room, he pushed against the door and called to the Serpent of the Sea: "Oh, Kólowissi! It is I, who speak to thee, O Serpent of the Sea I, thy priest. Let, I pray thee, let my child come to me again, and I will make atonement for her errors. Release her, though she has been so foolish, for she is thine, absolutely thine. But let her return once more to us that we may make atonement to thee more amply." So prayed the priest to the Serpent of the Sea.

When he had done this the great Serpent loosened his coils, and as he did so the whole building shook violently, and all the villagers became aware of the event, and trembled with fear.

The maiden at once awoke and cried piteously to her father for help.

"Come and release me, oh, my father! Come and release me!" she cried.

As the coils loosened she found herself able to rise. No sooner had she done this than the great Serpent bent the folds of his large coils nearest the doorway upward so that they formed an arch. Under this, filled with terror, the girl passed. She was almost stunned with the dread din of the monster's scales rasping past one another with a noise like the sound of flints trodden under the feet of a rapid runner, and once away from the writhing mass of coils, the poor maiden ran like a frightened deer out of the doorway, down the ladder and into the room below, casting herself on the breast of her mother.

But the priest still remained praying to the Serpent; and he ended his prayer as he had begun it, saying: "It shall be even as I have said; she shall be thine!"

He then went away and called the two warrior priest-chiefs of the town, and these called together all the other priests in sacred council. Then they performed the solemn ceremonies of the sacred rites--preparing plumes, prayer-wands, and offerings of treasure.

After four days of labor, these things they arranged and consecrated to the Serpent of the Sea. On that morning the old priest called his daughter and told her she must make ready to take these sacrifices and yield them up, even with herself, --most precious of them all, --to the great Serpent of the Sea; that she must yield up also all thoughts of her people and home forever, and go hence to the house of the great Serpent of the Sea, even in the Waters of the World. "For it seems," said he, "to have been your desire to do thus, as manifested by your actions.

You used even the sacred water for profane purposes; now this that I have told you is inevitable. Come; the time when you must prepare yourself to depart is near at hand."

She went forth from the home of her childhood with sad cries, clinging to the neck of her mother and shivering with terror. In the plaza, amidst the lamentations of all the people, they dressed her in her sacred cotton robes of ceremonial, embroidered elaborately, and adorned her with earrings, bracelets, beads, --many beautiful, precious things.

They painted her cheeks with red spots as if for a dance; they made a road of sacred meal toward the Door of the Serpent of the Sea--a distant spring in our land known to this day as the Doorway to the Serpent of the Sea--four steps toward this spring did they mark in sacred terraces on the ground at the western way of the plaza.

And when they had finished the sacred road, the old priest, who never shed one tear, although all the villagers wept sore, --for the maiden was very beautiful, --instructed his daughter to go forth on the terraced road, and, standing there, call the Serpent to come to her.

Then the door opened, and the Serpent descended from the high room where he was coiled, and, without using ladders, let his head and breast down to the ground in great undulations. He placed his head on the shoulder of the maiden, and the word was given-the word: "It is time"--and the maiden slowly started toward the west, cowering beneath her burden; but whenever she staggered with fear and weariness and was like to wander from the way, the Serpent gently pushed her onward and straightened her course.

Thus they went toward the river trail and in it, on and over the Mountain of the Red Paint; yet still the Serpent was not all uncoiled from the maiden's room in the house, but continued to crawl forth until they were past the mountain-- when the last of his length came forth. Here he began to draw himself together again and to assume a new shape. So that ere long his serpent form contracted, until, lifting his head from the maiden's shoulder, he stood up, in form a beautiful youth in sacred gala attire! He placed the scales of his serpent form, now small, under his flowing mantle, and called out to the maiden in a hoarse, hissing voice: "Let us speak one to the other. Are you tired, girl?" Yet she never moved her head, but plodded on with her eyes cast down.

"Are you weary, poor maiden?"--then he said in a gentler voice, as he arose erect and fell a little behind her, and wrapped his scales more closely in his blanket--and he was now such a splendid and brave hero, so magnificently dressed! And he repeated, in a still softer voice: "Are you still weary, poor maiden?"

At first she dared not look around, though the voice, so changed, sounded so far behind her and thrilled her wonderfully with its kindness. Yet she still felt the weight on her shoulder, the weight of that dreaded Serpent's head; for you know after one has carried a heavy burden on his shoulder or back, if it be removed he does not at once know that it is taken away; it seems still to oppress and pain him. So it was with her; but at length she turned around a little and saw a young man-a brave and handsome young man.

"May I walk by your side?" said he, catching her eye. "Why do you not speak with me?"

"I am filled with fear and sadness and shame," said she.

"Why?" asked he. "What do you fear?"

"Because I came with a fearful creature forth from my home, and he rested his head upon my shoulder, and even now I feel his presence there," said she, lifting her hand to the place where his head had rested, even still fearing that it might be there."

"But I came all the way with you," said he, "and I saw no such creature as you describe."

Upon this she stopped and turned back and looked again at him, and said: "You came all the way? I wonder where this fearful being has gone!"

He smiled, and replied: "I know where he has gone."

"Ah, youth and friend, will he now leave me in peace," said she, "and let me return to the home of my people?"

"No," replied he, "because he thinks very much of you."

"Why not? Where is he?"

"He is here," said the youth, smiling, and laying his hand on his own heart. "I am he."

"You are he?" cried the maiden. Then she looked at him again, and would not believe him. "Yea, my maiden, I am he!" said he. And he drew forth from under his flowing mantle the shriveled serpent scales, and showed them as proofs of his word. It was wonderful and beautiful to the maiden to see that he was thus, a gentle being; and she looked at him long.

Then he said: "Yes, I am he. I love you, my maiden! Will you not haply come forth and dwell with me? Yes, you will go with me, and dwell with me, and I will dwell with you, and I will love you. I dwell not now, but ever, in all the Waters of the World, and in each particular water. In all and each you will dwell with me forever, and we will love each other."

Behold! As they journeyed on, the maiden quite forgot that she had been sad; she forgot her old home, and followed and descended with him into the Doorway of the Serpent of the Sea and dwelt with him ever after.

It was thus in the days of the ancients. Therefore, the ancients, no less than ourselves, avoided using springs, except for the drinking of their water; for to this day we hold the flowing springs the most precious things on earth, and therefore use them not for any profane purposes whatsoever.

Thus shortens my story.

A Native American Prayer for Peace

O Great Spirit of our Ancestors, I raise my pipe to you.
To your messengers the four winds,
and to Mother Earth who provides for your children.
Give us the wisdom to teach our children to love, to
respect,
and to be kind to each other so that they may grow with
peace in mind.
Let us learn to share all the good things you provide for us
on this Earth.
- U.N. Day of Prayer for World Peace 2

About the Author and Artist

Thanks for choosing this book, if you enjoyed it, please leave positive feedback.

G.W. Mullins is an Author, Photographer, and Entrepreneur of Native American / Cherokee decent. He has been a published author for over 5 years. His writing has focused on the paranormal and Native American studies. Mullins has released several books on the history/stories/fables of the Native American Indians. Among his books are the extremely successful The Native American Story Book - Stories Of The American Indians For Children Volumes 1-5, The Native American Cookbook, and Walking With Spirits Native American Myths, Legends, And Folklore Volumes 1 Thru 6.

He has released books one and two in his Sci/fi Fantasy Series "From The Dead Of Night" series, including the Best-Selling titles - Daniel Is Waiting, and Daniel Returns. His most recent work includes the new series Rise Of The Snow Queen Book One The Polar Bear King and Messages from The Other Side a nonfiction book about communication with the dead.

For further information, on the writing, visit G.W. Mullins' web site at http://gwmullins.wix.com/officialsite.

C.L. Hause is an Illustrator / Artist who possesses a Master Of Fine Arts Degree specializing in Studio Art. He was the winner of the 2013 Johnny Hart Memorial Award as well of several others. He has always been inspired by nature, primitive and Native American design. He has released several books of his art including *"The Native American Art Book – Art Inspired By Native American Myths And Legends."*

For further information, on his art, visit C.L. Hause's web site at https://clhauseart.wixsite.com/officialpage

Also Available From G.W. Mullins and C.L. Hause

Daniel Awakens A Ghost Story Begins– From The Dead Of Night Prequel

Daniel Is Waiting A Ghost Story – From The Dead Of Night Book One

Daniel Returns A Ghost Story - From The Dead Of Night Book Two

Rise Of The Snow Queen Book One The Polar Bear King

Messages From The Other Side Stories of the Dead, Their Communication, and Unfinished Business

Vengeance

Mysteries Of The Unseen World – Ghost, Hauntings and The Unexplained

Haunted America Stories Of Ghost, Hauntings And The Unexplained

Timeless – A Paranormal Murder Mystery

Star People, Sky Gods, And Other Tales Of The Native American Indians

Walking With Spirits Native American Myths, Legends, And Folklore Volumes One Thru Six

The Native American Cookbook

Native American Cooking - An Indian Cookbook With Legends And Folklore

The Native American Story Book - Stories Of The American Indians For Children Volumes One Thru Five

The Best Native American Stories For Children

Cherokee A Collection of American Indian Legends, Stories And Fables

Creation Myths - Tales Of The Native American Indians

Strange Tales Of The Native American Indians

Spirit Quest - Stories Of The Native American Indians

Animal Tales Of The Native American Indians

Medicine Man - Shamanism, Natural Healing, Remedies And Stories Of The Native American Indians

Native American Legends: Stories Of The Hopi Indians Volumes One and Two

Totem Animals Of The Native Americans

The Best Native American Myths, Legends And Folklore Volumes One Thru Three

Ghosts, Spirits And The Afterlife In Native American Indian Mythology And Folklore

War Song: Tales Of The Native American Indians

Origin Tales Of The Native American Indians

CPSIA information can be obtained
at www.ICGtesting.com
Printed in the USA
BVHW041038210420
578018BV00016B/937

9 781645 709589